EDDIE AND THE FAIRY GODPUPPY

WEEKLY READER BOOKS PRESENTS

EDDIE

AND THE
FAIRY GODPUPPY

by Willo Davis Roberts

ILLUSTRATED BY LESLIE MORRILL

Atheneum   1984   New York

This book is a presentation of Weekly Reader Books.
Weekly Reader Books offers book clubs for children from
preschool through high school.

For further information write to:
Weekly Reader Books
4343 Equity Drive
Columbus, Ohio 43228

Library of Congress Cataloging in Publication Data

Roberts, Willo Davis.
Eddie and the fairy godpuppy.

Summary: Eddie, an orphan, hopes the puppy he finds is a fairy
godpuppy that will bring him a family and a real home.
[1. Orphans—Fiction.   2. Dogs—Fiction]   I. Morrill, Leslie, ill.
II. Title.
PZ7.R54465Ed   1984   [Fic]   83-15678
ISBN 0-689-31021-8

Text copyright © 1984 by Willo Davis Roberts
Pictures copyright © 1984 by Leslie H. Morrill
Published simultaneously in Canada by
McClelland & Stewart, Ltd.
Composition by Dix Type Inc., Syracuse, New York
Printed and bound by Fairfield Graphics,
Fairfield, Pennsylvania
Designed by Mary Ahern
First Edition

ONE

The sign in front said RIVERPARK CHILDREN'S HOME, but it didn't fool Eddie.

"An orphanage, that's what it is," he said to Miss Susan, who had a sign just like it, only smaller, on her desk. "I'll be stuck here forever, in an orphanage." He had picked some daisies from the field next door, and he stuck them in the little green vase beside her name sign.

Miss Susan was a pretty lady with brown hair who smiled a lot. She looked up at him and shook her head.

"Oh, Eddie, you know that Mrs. Wilson established the home to take care of children on a temporary basis, until permanent homes can be found for them, or they can rejoin their own families. I don't think you'll be here so long, dear. Two boys left last week to go into lovely homes."

Eddie rattled the marbles in his pocket. "That won't happen to me, though. Nobody's going to adopt me. Nobody likes me. I'm too ugly. They don't even want me in a foster home."

Miss Susan laughed and ruffled his hair with her fingers. Eddie liked it when she did that, though he never let it show. He remembered his grandma had done it, before she died.

"Oh, Eddie," Miss Susan said, "stop feeling sorry for yourself. You're not ugly at all. Why don't you go and tell Cook I said you might have some bread and jelly?"

Eddie sighed. Eating wasn't as good as being adopted, but it was the best he could do. He left Miss Susan's office and wandered down the hallway. In the glass-fronted bookcases there he could see his own reflection; he stopped and scowled at it. Red hair standing in stiff bristles, a short nose sprinkled with freckles; no wonder nobody wanted him. Who'd pick out a boy who looked like that?

He kicked at the reflection, but not too hard. Miss Susan would probably wallop him if he broke the glass. Jonas came in the front door in time to see him and stood watching, hands in his pockets.

"What did you do that for?" Jonas wanted to know.

Jonas had been at the Riverpark Children's Home almost as long as Eddie had. Nobody had adopted Jonas, either. Jonas said it was because he was black, but Miss Susan said some black family would come along one of these days and decide Jonas was exactly what they were looking for.

"I hate the way I look," Eddie said, sticking his hands in his pockets the way Jonas was doing. Jonas was nine, and he was quite a bit taller than Eddie, who was the same age. "I've been here six months, and nobody wants me. I'm homely."

"You can't help what you look like," Jonas said. "Or that your mother didn't want you."

"It hurts," Eddie said, his voice gruff, "when your mother doesn't want you. If my own mother didn't, why should anybody else?"

"My mom didn't want me, either," Jonas reminded him. "Miss Susan says some people are sick, and they can't help it if they don't want their kids. Come on, let's go play ball."

"It's too hot to run. Listen, Miss Susan said to tell Cook I could have bread and jelly. Cook won't know if she meant just me or both of us. Let's get something to eat."

"OK," Jonas agreed. "I hope Mrs. Mundy isn't in the kitchen."

Mrs. Mundy was in charge of the cooking and the housekeeping, and when Miss Susan wasn't around, she acted as if she had charge of the kids, too. None of the kids liked her at all, because she was big and fat and mean, and her voice was always cross.

Mrs. Mundy never thought the kids needed snacks, but she didn't argue with Miss Susan. She was there, talking to Cook, and she frowned, but she didn't stop the boys from coming in when Eddie told her he had permission to have bread and jelly.

Cook was tinkering with the dials on her table radio, making floury fingermarks on the dark plastic. She looked around and spoke to Mrs. Mundy. "It just stopped playing all of a sudden. I suppose I'll have to take it to the repair shop."

"It's probably got a loose tube," Eddie said. "You move it around all the time, and they jiggle loose."

Cook and Mrs. Mundy frowned at him. Eddie was used to that. Except for Miss Susan, everybody frowned when he said anything.

He reached out and gave the radio a hard

swat with the flat of his hand. Cook yelped and Mrs. Mundy reached for him, clamping her hand over his shoulder. He'd never understood how such a fat woman could have such thin, sharp fingers.

Cook started to reach for him, too, and then both women stopped. The radio had begun to play, the loud, fast music that Cook liked.

They looked at each other, speechless.

"Loose tube," Eddie confirmed, and got his bread and jelly. Nobody asked if Jonas had permission, too.

They took their sandwiches outside and walked across the grass toward where some of the other kids were playing ball. They sat down in the shade of the apple tree and ate, wishing they had something to drink, without going back to the house for it.

"I guess the river water isn't clean enough to drink," Eddie said, licking at a sticky place on his hand.

"You know the rules. They get real mad if you go near the river, even if you can swim. Can you swim?"

"Sure. We lived by a lake, once. Before my grandma died."

"I can swim, too," Jonas said. "There was a

pool in the town where I lived," Jonas said. "I never had a grandma."

Eddie looked at him. "Doesn't everybody have to have a grandma? Even if they don't know them?"

"Well, sure. I meant I didn't know any grandma," Jonas said. He scraped a glob of jelly off his pants and ate it, then sucked the finger. "Oh, shoot, look who's coming this way."

Arnie hadn't been playing ball, only watching the others. He was walking toward the boys, pausing to pull Cheryl's pigtail as he walked past her. The little girl struck at him, and Arnie laughed.

Arnie was ten, and he wasn't an orphan at all, so he didn't have to worry about anybody adopting him. He was here because his parents had been in an accident and there was no one else to take care of him. Mrs. Wilson, the lady they seldom saw but who paid for everything here, didn't care why a child needed a home. As long as he *did*, she had given orders to her staff to make that child welcome. Arnie'd be going home as soon as his mother and father were out of the hospital.

Eddie hoped that would be soon, because

Arnie sometimes wasn't very nice. He was always making remarks that hurt someone else's feelings. Miss Susan, who was always nice to everybody, said it was because Arnie himself was feeling lost and lonely, but Eddie didn't understand why that should make him want everybody else to be miserable, too.

He stopped now, looking down at the pair sitting under the apple tree. "What's the matter, nobody wanted you two on their team?" he asked, grinning.

"No, is that why you're not playing?" Jonas responded.

Arnie stopped grinning. He didn't like it when the remarks were made by anyone else. "You make a funny-looking couple of buddies," he said. "Eddie's skin is so pale, except for those stupid freckles, and Jonas's is so dark. Like salt and pepper," he said, and the grin came back. "Yeah, salt and pepper. That's what I'm going to call you from now on. Salt and pepper."

They both stared at him in disgust, and after a few minutes Arnie walked away, chanting, "Salt and Pepper, go together! Black and white and brains like a feather!"

Eddie grunted. "Not much of a poet, is he?"

"No," Jonas agreed. "I suppose he'll have everybody in the place calling us that. We ought to think up a poem of our own. Let's see, Arnie, Arnie, lives in a barny! What I think is, he's pretty corny! How's that, as good as his?"

Eddie laughed. "Yeah! Come on, let's go get a drink. I sure wish they'd let us play by the river. It'd be nice and cool to wade out in it and swim."

"It's not a very big river, or very deep. I don't think it's dangerous, but Miss Susan gets upset if we go there. Maybe we could wet each other down with the hose."

Eddie sprang to his feet. "Good! Let's go do it," he said, and they raced across the grass toward the big house.

Jonas won, as he usually did, because his legs were longer, though Eddie wasn't far behind. They slapped their hands against the house as if it were the finish line for the race, and then, laughing, went on around the corner of the building to find the garden hose.

The hose was there, all right, but they stopped short, staring. There was a man with a ladder and some buckets and a big canvas tarp that he was spreading out on the grass.

Eddie looked at the buckets. "Exterior

Paint," he read slowly. He raised his eyes to the man, who wore white coveralls with lovely speckles of paint all over them, all different colors.

"What's *exterior?*" asked Eddie.

"Means to be used on the outside," the man said, giving him only a glance before he began to pry up the lid of one of the pails.

"You going to paint the whole place?" Eddie demanded, edging close enough to look into the pail. The paint was a sort of tan; Eddie and Jonas exchanged disappointed glances. "Kind of a stupid color for a big house."

The man looked at the paint, thought it over, and nodded. "Not very pretty at that, is it? But that's what they want." He leaned the ladder against the side of the house and poured some paint into a smaller pail. "Who're you fellows?"

"I'm Eddie, and this is my friend Jonas." Eddie looked at him interestedly, thinking that the pale blue on the bib of the coveralls would have been a much prettier color for the house. "Who're you?"

"Mr. Caw." The man dipped his brush into the paint and swiped it experimentally across the boards. "You say it twice," he said.

"Caw Caw," Jonas said, and the boys both grinned. "Like a crow. Mr. Caw Caw." The painter wasn't smiling, but they decided it was a joke.

They didn't hear Mrs. Mundy coming, but when her fingers closed on his shoulder for the second time that day, Eddie knew who it was.

"Don't you get in that painter's way and mess things up," she said. "Are they bothering you, Mr. Caw?"

"Oh, they're pests, all right," said Mr. Caw, "but I can handle them."

"No need for that. I'll keep them out from under your feet," Mrs. Mundy said. She dug her fingers into Jonas's shoulder, too, and pushed them ahead of her toward the back of the house.

Eddie looked over his shoulder, which wasn't easy to do the way she was holding him. "Goodbye, Mr. Caw Caw!"

Mrs. Mundy frowned and shook him, shaking Jonas at the same time. "Don't you go being fresh to your elders, young man. Now you go along and play and don't make a nuisance of yourselves."

They stepped over the hose, not daring to try to do anything with it while Mrs. Mundy was around. Even when she went inside, they thought maybe they'd better find something else to do.

"Jonas!"

They turned at the voice behind them to see Miss Susan coming around the corner. "I have a letter here about you," she said, waving an envelope. "From a Mrs. Castle."

Eddie saw how his friend's face lit up. "The Castles were our next door neighbors until they moved away. They have six kids, and we always had a lot of fun playing in their backyard," Jonas told him.

"They've just learned about your being here," Miss Susan said. "They want to come and see you, and they've asked if they might take you home with them for a visit."

Jonas's grin almost split his face in half. "I can go, can't I?"

"Yes, of course. We'll write and tell them to come. They live a hundred miles away, so they may not get here right away, but we'll find out. Would you like to come and help me compose the letter?"

Eddie was left on his own. He was glad for Jonas; maybe the Castle family would decide to be foster parents for him, if they didn't want to adopt him. A family that had six kids already probably wouldn't need to adopt another one.

Eddie had been in one foster home and he hadn't liked it much, but some of the other kids had gone to foster homes and said it was as good as being part of a family of their own.

It was nicer here than in the foster home. Here he at least had Miss Susan when things got too bad; she always listened to him and made him feel better.

Well, if Jonas wasn't around to talk to, he might as well read, Eddie thought. He got his book out of its hiding place under the back steps and cut across the lawn toward the river.

There was a fence that the kids weren't supposed to go past, but the best place to read without being bothered by Arnie was in the apple tree just beyond the home boundaries. Eddie climbed over the fence, and just as he'd suspected, it was cooler there. He didn't want to upset Miss Susan, so he wouldn't get near the water, but he didn't see any reason why he shouldn't be cool. He climbed up into the tree and opened his book.

It was one of his favorites, about a little boy

who was like himself in that he had no home and no mother or father. The little boy was lame, and he was locked in a tower, where he was very lonely. Eddie skipped the beginning, because he knew it by heart anyway, and got to the part he liked best. That was where the fairy godmother came and brought the little boy a magic carpet.

Eddie nodded, leaning against the tree trunk, dreaming in the shade. He wished there were still such things as fairy godmothers. He sure needed one. Otherwise he'd never get out of this blamed orphanage, not even into a foster home.

The book and the daydream blended, and he thought he was with his fairy godmother, who looked like Miss Susan.

The next thing he knew, the sun-dappled leaves were spinning around and the ground came up to meet him with a smack. One arm was twisted underneath him, and it hurt something awful.

TWO

The pain in Eddie's arm was fierce. He sat up, and in spite of all he could do, the tears began to slide down his cheeks.

"Ow! Oh, Ow!" Eddie moaned, squeezing his eyes tight shut. And then suddenly the tears were wiped away by something warm and moist and rough. A tongue!

Eddie opened his eyes, and for a moment he forgot how much his arm hurt. It was a dog, a little brown dog with short hair and a stubby tail that wagged as the animal looked at him.

The dog licked him again, this time on his uninjured arm, and Eddie said, "Where did you come from?"

A few minutes before he'd fallen asleep and tumbled out of the tree, he'd had a view of the whole field this side of the Riverpark Children's Home, all the way to the river, and there hadn't been a dog anywhere in sight. Was it magic?

He felt dizzy, and he drew in a deep breath. No, it couldn't be magic. Could it?

Out in the river an old tin wash tub settled slowly to the bottom as the water filled it. Eddie didn't see it, and even if he had, he wouldn't have realized that the little dog had been set afloat in a leaky tub by a trio of thoughtless boys. The little dog couldn't tell him how he'd got there, and though his feet were wet when he put them on Eddie's knee, Eddie was too shaken to think what that might mean.

Boy, his arm was sure aching.

"Hey, there, you all right?"

Eddie turned and saw the painter, Mr. Caw, coming across the field. The kids had stopped playing ball and most of them were coming, too. The dog licked Eddie's face again, and Eddie hoped that nobody could tell he'd been a crybaby, just for a minute.

Mr. Caw wasn't used to running. He was breathing heavily by the time he reached the shade under the apple tree. He looked at the dog. "Where'd he come from?"

"I think he's magic," Eddie said. "He just suddenly appeared. I was thinking about fairy godmothers and wishing I had one, and all of a sudden *he* was here."

"You got your wish, eh?" Mr. Caw chuckled.

"No, I didn't wish for a *dog,*" Eddie said scornfully. "I wished for a fairy godmother. To help me get out of this place."

Mr. Caw looked at the dog, who was wagging his stumpy tail and licking the last of the jelly off Eddie's fingers.

"Maybe he's your fairy godpuppy," Mr. Caw suggested.

Eddie stared at him. Mr. Caw looked perfectly serious.

The other kids were almost there, though some of them had dropped back since it was plain Eddie hadn't killed himself in the fall. If he'd been bleeding, probably they'd all have come to look at him.

Eddie looked back at Mr. Caw. "There isn't any such thing as a fairy godpuppy," he said.

"There is so," Mr. Caw contradicted.

Eddie eyed him suspiciously. Grown people were always telling you not to tell lies, and then they did it themselves. The painter didn't look as if he were lying, though.

Eddie dropped his hand, the one that didn't hurt, onto the dog's back, and the puppy squirmed happily.

"He looks like an ordinary dog," Eddie said. "How can you tell if he's a fairy godpuppy?"

"You said he was magic. He came out of nowhere, didn't he? Ordinary dogs come walking up the road. He came when you needed help, didn't he? When you fell out of the tree?"

That was so. And Mr. Caw didn't know about the tears being licked away. Eddie would have considered himself disgraced if anyone had seen him crying, though Miss Susan said there was nothing wrong with crying when you really needed to.

"I wonder if he *is* magic," Eddie said hopefully. It would be great to have a dog of his own, but a fairy godpuppy! That would be super!

Then he remembered. "We can't have dogs. Mrs. Mundy doesn't like them."

Mr. Caw raised his eyebrows. "Doesn't like dogs! What sort of person doesn't like dogs?"

"She's allergic to them. They make her sneeze, and she says they're dirty."

"Oh. That's a shame." The painter cleared his throat. "That arm hurting you, boy?"

"Some," Eddie admitted. It didn't hurt quite as bad now, but it was painful enough so that he didn't want to move it.

"Let's get you inside and have somebody take a look at it. Twisted kind of funny, seems like."

"What about . . ." He just had time to say the words before all the kids got there. "What about the fairy godpuppy?"

"I have a cheese sandwich left in my lunch pail," said Mr. Caw. "I think fairy godpuppies are very fond of cheese sandwiches."

And sure enough, he was.

"When Miss Susan said a boy with a broken arm," said the doctor, "I knew it must be Eddie. How come you're the only one in this home ever breaks a bone, Eddie?"

"Because he's the only one who goes to sleep in the apple tree," Miss Susan said, laughing.

"And the only one climbs on the roof after cats," said Mrs. Mundy. She wasn't amused at all.

"And the only one who thinks he can walk a tightrope on the clothesline," added Cook.

The arm didn't hurt much, now that it was encased in a fresh white cast. Dr. Holmes had taken him to the hospital to x-ray his arm, and then put on the cast and dropped him off at the children's home before he went on to have his own dinner. Eddie had a sling to hold up the arm, because with the cast on it, it was heavy.

"Thank you, Doctor," Miss Susan said, and gave Eddie a hug. "You can go now, Eddie. It feels better, doesn't it?"

"For mercy's sake," Mrs. Mundy warned, "stay out of trouble."

Eddie muttered, "Yes, ma'am," to both of them, and went out to show his cast to Mr. Caw, who was putting the lids back on his paint cans.

"Pretty nice," said Mr. Caw admiringly. "Can I be the first to autograph it?"

"What's autograph?" Eddie asked.

"Why, you know. Sign your name. Didn't you have your friends sign their names on your other casts?"

He hadn't, but it sounded like a good idea.

"In paint," he suggested. "Everybody else will use a pencil or ink, but one in paint, that would be special."

Mr. Caw looked doubtfully at the tan paint he was using.

"We don't like this, do we? Tell you what, there's a little blue left in a can in my truck. How would that be?"

He had to hunt for a little tiny paint brush, and he printed "Good luck from Mr. Caw Caw," in bright blue letters. "Now," he said, "what are we going to do about your fairy godpuppy?"

Jonas had showed up to watch the autographing. "I think he wants out of your truck, Mr. Caw. He's whining."

"Let him out, then," the painter said.

When Eddie opened the pickup door, Jonas said, "Oh, oh!"

It seemed that fairy godpuppies were very much like ordinary puppies in some ways. This one had chewed the brim off Mr. Caw's cap.

"Hmmm." Mr. Caw looked at the pup. "Maybe he's not a fairy godpuppy, after all."

"If he's magic," Eddie said hopefully, "maybe he wouldn't make Mrs. Mundy sneeze. Maybe he could make her like him."

Mr Caw coughed a little before he could speak. "Well, he's a little young to be really good at magic. Maybe it would be better to keep him out of sight for a day or so until he thinks of something. I'll ask around and see if anybody I know can keep a dog, if you can't keep him here. You got any place you could hide him until tomorrow?"

Eddie thought. "Under my bed, I guess."

Mr. Caw frowned, but it wasn't the same kind of frown everybody else used on Eddie. "That sounds sort of risky. You can't walk through the halls carrying him, and if you get caught with him inside, you'll be in a lot of trouble."

Eddie thought of a way to get the puppy upstairs, but he remembered just in time that Mr. Caw was a grownup and maybe not completely dependable. "We'll think of something," he told the painter, who smiled.

"Good. Out in a shed, or something like that." He began to pack up his cans and brushes and rolled up the tarp that was keeping the paint off the grass. "How come you need a fairy god-puppy so bad?" he wanted to know.

"I want to get out of this orphanage," Eddie explained. "And nobody will ever adopt me."

"Oh? Why not?"

"Because," Eddie said earnestly, "I'm so homely. Nobody likes red-headed, freckled, homely boys."

"You are kind of a pickle, at that, comes to looks, aren't you? Still," Mr. Caw said, "it takes more than looks to be the pick of the crop, you know. What kind of person you are, inside, and the things you do, that's more important than what you look like."

"Yeah," Jonas agreed, nodding. "And Eddie's my best friend in this place."

Eddie kicked at a clump of grass. "Mrs. Mundy always tells people what kind of boy I am. She says I'm a pesky nuisance. She tells them how I'm always tearing my clothes and I wrecked her watch—I didn't really, I only took it apart and it needed a new spring, the old one was broken; but she said it was my fault—and she says I run away, because I don't hear them when they call. . . ." He took a deep breath and finished up in a rush, "And she says I'm a roughneck because I knocked Lonnie down, only it was an accident! She never believes me!"

Mr. Caw added solemnly. "I can see you have a problem. Yep, you sure do need a fairy godpuppy, all right. Only maybe this isn't the time for you to have one, with Mrs. Mundy's allergies and all. You find a box for him in that shed out back, son, and I'll see if I can find a place for him to stay until you get out of this place."

Eddie shook his head. "Without some help,

I'll never get out," he said gloomily. "But we'll find a place for him, won't we, Jonas?"

"Sure," Jonas said, though by his face Eddie could tell Jonas didn't think they'd be able to hide the dog from Mrs. Mundy for very long.

"Uh," Eddie began, as Mr. Caw began to load things into the back of the truck, "could we borrow that big empty bucket? If you don't need it for anything?"

Mr. Caw gave him a funny look but he didn't ask what it was for. It wasn't until he'd driven away that Jonas asked.

"What're we going to do with it?"

"We're going to put the dog in it and tie a rope to the handle and lift him up to the window." Eddie pointed upward, to where a window opened right near his own bed. "Then Mrs. Mundy won't see him."

Jonas looked uncertain. "Mrs. Mundy'll be mad if she finds him. She might even hurt him."

"We'll just have to make sure she doesn't find him, then," Eddie said. "Come on, are you going to help me get a rope? We'll take that clothesline."

The puppy was small enough to sit in the big pail with only his head sticking over the top.

He didn't like it much, though; he whined and scratched at the inside of the pail, trying to get out.

"Listen," Eddie told him, putting his face close to the dog's so that it would pay attention. "You're going to have to be quiet so nobody hears you. If you're magic, you ought to be smart enough to know that, even if you aren't very old."

The puppy stopped whining and wagged his tail, and Eddie grunted in satisfaction. "OK, then. Jonas, you want to be the one takes him in, upstairs, or the one that stays down here and makes sure he's in the pail when it goes up? You'll have to tie a good strong knot, to make sure it doesn't break loose and let him fall."

"I can tie good knots," Jonas assured him. "You go inside and drop the rope down."

To Eddie's horror, he met Arnie at the corner of the house. Arnie looked at the rope coiled over Eddie's arm.

"What are you going to do with that? Tie up old Mrs. Mundy so she can't keep pestering you?" Arnie asked.

If Arnie knew what the rope was for, would he tell? Eddie didn't know, and he couldn't take the chance. Eddie swung the length of clothesline back and forth, pretending that it was not important. "I would, but I don't think there's enough of it to go all the way around her," he said, and kept on walking.

Behind him, Arnie laughed. "Too bad," he said. "Think of all the things we could do, if Mrs. Mundy was tied up."

Eddie climbed the stairs, hoping he wouldn't meet anyone else who wanted to know what the rope was for. Especially Mrs. Mundy! She'd never believe him, no matter what he said, and she'd probably take the rope away from him.

There was no one in the big dormitory where the younger boys slept. There were eight beds, and Eddie's was the one nearest the window at the far end of the room.

Eddie pushed the window up as far as it would go and unlatched the screen to push that out of the way. He dropped one end of the rope down to Jonas, whose dark face stared up at him, waiting.

Eddie's heart was beating very fast. He looked over his shoulder, in case anyone had come in behind him. The big room was still

empty, and he leaned out the window and called softly to his friend below.

"OK," he told Jonas. "Send him up."

Eddie squeezed his eyes shut and hoped, very hard, that this would work and they wouldn't get caught. If there was any chance at all that the puppy really was a magic one, he had to figure out some way to keep him, Eddie thought.

Just then he felt the tug against the rope, and he began to pull up the big bucket with the dog in it. It wasn't easy with his left arm in a cast and only his fingers sticking out the end. The pail bumped against the side of the house, and the puppy whined again in fear.

The edge of the bucket caught on the window frame, and for a minute Eddie was afraid he wasn't going to get the puppy inside, after all. He'd been wrapping the rope around his casted elbow as he drew it in, and it was a good thing, because he nearly dropped the pail before he could haul it inside.

If the puppy hadn't helped him by reaching out to lick his face and then scrambling out of the big bucket, over the windowsill, Eddie didn't know what would have happened. He was so relieved that the dog was safely inside that he forgot about the pail and the clothesline. The next thing he knew the rope was sliding away and he heard Jonas yelp about the same time he heard the pail hitting the ground. At least he hoped the ground was all that had been hit.

Eddie hugged the dog to him and leaned out the window. "You all right, Jonas?" he asked.

"Yeah," Jonas said, but he was shaking his head. "Only the bucket fell in the flower bed and smashed all those flowers. I better hide it in the shed, OK?"

"OK," Eddie agreed. "Then come on up and help me figure out what to do next, all right?"

The fairy godpuppy was squirming so hard, trying to lick Eddie's face, that it was all Eddie could do to hold him. It felt funny, and he started to laugh.

And then he suddenly didn't feel like laughing at all, because someone was coming. He heard footsteps in the hallway, and just in the nick of time he crouched down between the beds and hoped that whoever it was wouldn't come into the room.

THREE

Mrs. Mundy's voice boomed through the dormitory. "I thought I heard someone in here. Is anybody here?"

Eddie pressed himself flat on the floor in the space between the beds, holding the fairy godpuppy down with his good arm. The dog made no sound and licked at his ear. It tickled, only Eddie couldn't tell him to stop.

"Funny," Mrs. Mundy said. "I was sure I heard something. Didn't you hear it?"

The other voice was Cheryl's. "No, I didn't hear anything. Please, may I have a Band-aid before the blood gets on my dress?"

Mrs. Mundy made a grouchy sound. Under the bed, Eddie could see her feet in big white shoes. If she came much farther into the room, she'd see him, too, for sure.

What would she do if she found him here with a dog?

She sneezed, and then blew her nose. "If you didn't do all those things the boys do, you wouldn't need Band-aids," she said in her usual cross manner. "Come along to the bathroom. I hope you're not all going to get as careless as that Eddie."

The big feet went away, and after a while, when he'd listened to Mrs. Mundy and Cheryl going back down the stairs, Eddie dared to start breathing again. He sat up, and the dog came into his lap to be petted.

"At least you were smart enough to keep still," Eddie said. "You'll always have to be quiet when anybody else is around, you know, or they'll find you and take you away. Maybe to the pound. Do you know what the pound is?"

The dog wagged his tail. He was very soft and warm against Eddie; he felt nicer than anything else Eddie could remember.

"All right, then. Can you do any magic? Can you get us out of here? Even into a foster home, if you can't get us adopted."

The dog seemed to know what he was saying; the brown eyes were very bright, and every time Eddie spoke the stumpy tail wagged. Eddie didn't know if the dog was agreeing to get them out or not, though. It might have been better to have a regular fairy godmother, who could talk.

"Eddie?" The voice was a loud whisper.

Eddie ducked his head to look under the bed and recognized the old blue and red running shoes belonging to Jonas.

"Over here," Eddie said, allowing his head to rise above the level of the bed. "Did you hide the bucket?"

Jonas crouched beside him, stretching out a hand to stroke the silky fur of the little dog. "I put it behind the shed. Nobody ever goes out there except Mr. Linders when he cuts the grass. When it fell, it mashed a lot of flowers." Jonas cleared his throat. "And scraped some of the new paint off the side of the house. They'll probably notice it."

"Maybe Mr. Caw will fix it before anybody else sees it," Eddie hoped aloud. "Mrs. Mundy almost caught us, but she had to put a bandage on Cheryl's finger."

Jonas nodded. "She cut it on a can. Maybe she'll have to have a shot. Listen, where are you going to keep this dog? We can't stay with him and watch him all the time."

"I thought under my bed. Do you think he's housebroke? So I can just take him outside a few times a day? Or will I have to hide him outside, the way Mr. Caw said?"

"He looks big enough to be housebroke. What are you going to call him?"

Eddie considered. "I don't suppose I'd better call him Fairy Godpuppy. It's a pretty long name."

Jonas was bright eyed with excitement. "Do you really think he's a magic dog?"

"He came out of nowhere, didn't he? How could he do that, if he wasn't magic?" Eddie didn't know if he really believed that or not, but he *wanted* to believe it. "Maybe I could use initials. Remember that boy who was only here a few days, the one named R.D.? I could call the puppy F.G.P. What do you think?"

They said it aloud a few times. F.G.P. It wasn't a usual sort of dog name, but when Eddie leaned down and spoke directly to the puppy, asking, "What do *you* think? Do you want to be F.G.P.?" the dog wagged his tail so wildly they decided that was it. They'd call him F.G.P., only they wouldn't tell anybody what the initials stood for. Just in case nobody else thought he was magic.

They found a cardboard box to put him in, one that Cook had gotten full of groceries. Jonas had seen it out by the trash burner and sneaked it inside before supper, when all the grownups were busy in the kitchen and dining room. One of the beds wasn't in use, and they took the pillow off that bed and put it in the bottom of the box: then they shoved it under Eddie's bed.

F.G.P. didn't like that at all. He whined and cried and scratched at the inside of the box, until Eddie lay flat and spoke to him very seriously. "You have to stay out of sight, or they'll send you away. Understand? We're going down to eat, but we'll be back with food for you as soon as we can. If you make any noise, somebody will hear you. So be quiet, OK?"

As they left the dormitory, Jonas said, "I don't think you made him understand too well, Eddie. He's still whining."

"As long as they can't hear him downstairs," Eddie muttered. "Mrs. Mundy probably won't come up here until bedtime, and by then I'll have food for him and be able to stay with him."

They had closed the door to the dormitory, and they didn't hear him as they went down the stairs. The others were already in the dining room, and the two slid into their places at the big table.

Once Eddie thought he heard barking, faint

and far off; he looked at Jonas, who heard it too. There was liver that night, which Eddie didn't care for, though he thought F.G.P. would like it. He rolled his up in a paper napkin when no one was watching and hid it inside the sling that held up his broken arm.

Jonas was saving food, too. He put half a roll in his pocket and a stalk of broccoli. Arnie saw him and frowned.

"What are you doing?"

"Saving myself a snack," Jonas said, and looked to make sure none of the adults heard him.

"Broccoli?" Arnie asked, disbelieving. "Here, you want mine, too?"

"Sure, if it'll go in my other pocket," Jonas agreed, and slid the vegetable between their plates and over the edge of the table.

When they got back upstairs, they offered F.G.P. the broccoli first, thinking he might eat it better while he was really hungry. He did, but he smelled out something better in Eddie's sling. He ate the liver very quickly and sniffed around for something more.

"Sorry, that's all there is for now. I wonder if he needs a drink?"

"We had a dog once," Jonas said, "and he had to have fresh water all the time. How we going to do that, Eddie? We can't take him in the bathroom; somebody might come along and see him. We'll have to find something to carry water in."

There was nothing in the boys' bathroom except a great big wastebasket, and they didn't see any way F.G.P. could drink out of that without drowning. Since there was no one around, they peeked into the girls' bathroom.

"Not much in here, either," Jonas said. "Should we try Mrs. Mundy's bathroom? Maybe she has something we could use."

Cook went home at night, the same as Miss Susan did, but Mrs. Mundy slept on the second floor along with the children. She had her own private room and her own bathroom. Her towels were pink instead of blue ones.

"Here," Eddie said, spotting a small container on the edge of the sink. "This is about the right size. What's it for, do you think?"

"For her false teeth. My uncle had one like that," Jonas explained, "because he took them out at night and left them soaking in a covered dish like that one. OK, let's use that."

They filled the container with water and carried it back to the dormitory. As soon as they opened the door, Eddie cried out.

"Hey! Are you trying to get us all in trouble, you stupid dog?"

They hadn't pushed the box back under the bed, and F.G.P. had climbed out of it. That wouldn't have been so bad except that he'd decided to chew on something, and what he'd chosen was one of Eddie's socks. When Eddie grabbed it, he saw holes from puppy teeth.

"For a magic dog, you aren't very smart," Eddie told him rather crossly. "They're always complaining how I tear my clothes climbing over fences and things. What are they going to think about this sock?"

He put the container of water down, and F.G.P. drank thirstily, that silly little tail wagging furiously all the time. It was hard to stay mad at him when he was so cute, and when he clearly appreciated everything they did for him.

"Are we going to hide him from the other kids?" Jonas wanted to know. "Or tell them about him?"

"Do you think any of them might tell on us?"

Jonas sat back on his heels, grinning when F.G.P. crawled into his lap and began to chew on a button.

"I don't know about Arnie. I bet nobody else would tell."

"Maybe I better try to keep him secret, for tonight anyway," Eddie decided. "If he's not hungry, maybe he won't make any noise but will stay asleep. I'll have to take him outside before we go to bed, though. Maybe we better do it now, before everybody else gets tired of watching TV and comes upstairs. You be the lookout and make sure nobody's around, and I'll take him downstairs."

They knew it was dangerous, using the stairs, but usually Mrs. Mundy watched television until it was time to get everybody ready for bed; then she'd come up and inspect them all to make sure they'd washed behind their ears and not left a mess in the bathrooms.

Jonas went cautiously down to the first floor. He peered into the living room, then turned to motion to Eddie to hurry. They both heaved a sigh of relief when they'd escaped outside.

F.G.P. didn't seem in any hurry to do his

business so they could take him inside again. He raced around their feet, jumping up and falling down in a silly way that made them both laugh.

They stopped laughing, though, before they started up to the second floor. Fortunately, whatever Mrs. Mundy and the kids were watching in the living room was funny, and as the boys reached the foot of the stairs there was a great wave of laughter, giving the boys a chance to hurry up out of sight.

They decided they'd better get ready for bed at once, taking turns watching F.G.P., so that they didn't have to leave him alone. Already it was clear that the puppy didn't like being by himself.

Eddie washed as best he could without using his left arm and wiped up most of the water from the bathroom floor. He took F.G.P. another drink, then returned the container to Mrs. Mundy's bathroom before she could discover that it was missing. Maybe tomorrow he'd find something else that he wouldn't have to remember to return between times.

As soon as they heard the others coming, they put F.G.P. into the box. "Remember, now, you have to be quiet," Eddie whispered, and turned on Arnie's radio to cover any small sounds the dog might make.

Mrs. Mundy came to the doorway, her heavy figure filling the space so they couldn't see beyond her. "You two ready for bed already? What's the matter? You sick?"

"My arm aches some," Eddie said, "and I'm tired." It wasn't a lie; it did ache, a little.

"If it hurts too much for you to sleep, the doctor said you could have an aspirin," Mrs. Mundy said, and for once she didn't sound cross at all.

"I think I can go to sleep," Eddie said. He hoped she wouldn't come any closer and that F.G.P. would stay very quiet. Even with the radio playing, Mrs. Mundy couldn't help hearing a dog if it whined or barked.

F.G.P. was quiet, perhaps because Jonas sat on his own bed next to Eddie's with one foot inside the box, rubbing the dog with his bare toes. Mrs. Mundy sneezed.

"Don't know what's in the air up here," she said. "Nobody brought any flowers in, did they? You know I'm allergic to some flowers."

Eddie and Jonas shook their heads. "No, no flowers," Jonas said soberly.

She sneezed again and blew her nose, then turned and walked out of the room, catching Arnie by the ear, as he tried to pass by her, to see if his neck was clean.

"Boy," Arnie said, coming into the room with one red ear, "I'll be glad when I get out of this place. Maybe I'll get to go home by the end of next week, Miss Susan says. Hey, how come my radio's on?"

"We didn't think you'd mind if we played it," Jonas said. "It's a neat radio."

Arnie flopped on his bed. "I got it from my grandpa for my birthday. You guys got grandpas?"

Both of them shook their heads. "I had a grandma," Eddie said, "but she died. That's why I came here."

Cary and Lonnie came in, each with one red ear. They started scuffling with each other and fell onto Lonnie's bed, laughing. Mrs. Mundy rapped sharply on the door frame.

"You'd better turn off the music," she told them. "Good night, now."

"Good night," they all chorused, and then they heard her at the door of the girls' dormitory. After that she went to watch television for a few more hours before she went to bed herself.

Arnie reached up and turned off his radio. He lay flat on the bed, and then sat up again. "What was that?"

"I didn't hear anything," Eddie said, and reached his good arm down over the edge of the bed to poke his fingers into the box. As soon as he touched F.G.P., the dog stopped whimpering.

"I didn't, either," Jonas said.

"I did," Lonnie said. Lonnie was the smallest of all of them, with dark curls that the ladies all loved to touch. Miss Susan said it wouldn't be long before one of them took him home with her. After all the paperwork had been done, of course. Miss Susan said there was a lot of paperwork to an adoption or a foster home, either one.

"I did, too," Cary agreed. Cary was six, the same as Lonnie, and everybody thought he was cute, too. He had freckles, but they weren't as dark as Eddie's, nor so numerous, and he didn't have red hair. "It sounded like a dog."

Arnie slid his feet to the floor. "It *is* a dog! You guys are hiding a dog! That's why you brought that stuff up here to eat! I *knew* nobody was crazy enough to save cold broccoli for a snack!"

Eddie's heart sank. He'd hoped to get through at least one night without being caught. He forgot to stroke the puppy's ears, and F.G.P. whined and then barked. There was no keeping him a secret now.

"Wow!" Arnie crossed the space between the beds and knelt to pull the box out from under the spread. "Where did you get him?"

"Hey, he's cute," Dick said, bouncing onto the bed beside Jonas. "What's his name?" Dick was Cheryl's brother, and he had the same thick blond hair that she did, only his wasn't in braids. Dick and Cheryl weren't worried about being adopted, either, because they had an aunt who was coming from California to get them, and they'd go live with her.

"F.G.P.," Eddie said, after a moment when he hoped with all his heart that nobody would tell on him.

"F.G.P.? What kind of silly name is that?" Arnie wanted to know. He put a hand into the box, and to Eddie's disappointment, F.G.P. licked at it the same as he would have done with Eddie himself.

"That's his name," Eddie said stubbornly. "F.G.P.."

"That's initials, not a name," Arnie said. He hauled the puppy out of the box and held him against the front of his pajamas. "What do they stand for?"

"Nothing," Eddie lied. He knew they'd make fun of him for believing he had a fairy godpuppy, a magic dog. "It's a name, like R.D."

"Let me hold him," Cary begged, and took him from Arnie. "Hey, he likes me! See, he's kissing me!"

Eddie watched as the dog licked at all of them, while each one petted him. Barry, the oldest boy in the room and the quietest, held him last and asked, "What are you going to do with him?"

"Keep him," Eddie said. "If nobody tells."

"We won't tell, will we, guys?" Lonnie asked. "Can we play with him, too, Eddie?"

"We'll help you save up food for him," Arnie said. "I've got a dog at home. Well, he's in a kennel, now, but I'll have him when I get back. His name's Jerry."

Eddie reached for his dog and was glad that he snuggled against him as if knowing whose dog he was. "You can help feed him and help keep him quiet, too. He's too young to know enough to be still."

"I'll give him my cauliflower, next time we have any," Cary offered.

Eddie slid back under the covers, taking F.G.P. with him. "I think he'll sleep better if he's close to me."

It took them all a while to calm down; they were excited about having a dog in the dormitory. F.G.P. went to sleep at once, curled against Eddie's side. After everything was quiet, Eddie shifted around so that it didn't hurt to feel the pressure of the cast.

"Please," he whispered very softly, so that only F.G.P. could hear. "Please be a real fairy godpuppy."

F.G.P. made a little snoring sound so Eddie guessed he hadn't heard. Eddie stroked the silky ears, until he, too, fell asleep.

FOUR

Eddie got up early the next morning so that he could take F.G.P. outside; but he was afraid to use the main stairs because Miss Susan and Mrs. Mundy were talking in the front hall.

The only thing he could do was sneak down the narrow, dark stairway that led to the kitchen area, which the children weren't supposed to use. The back door was usually locked, except when Cook was in the kitchen. Eddie was sure it would be open now, because Cook was there. He waited until he thought she was busy with her back turned and then dashed past the open doorway and onto the porch.

The puppy was quiet as long as someone held him or fed him. There was nothing left in the way of food, but Eddie hugged him against his chest and hurried out past the shed in the yard to a place where the dog could run for a few minutes.

The thought of going past Cook again, when she might turn at any minute and see

49

him, made Eddie uneasy. Which would be safer, to try to hide F.G.P. and go up the rear stairs, or to tie him out behind the shed until later?

Eddie was afraid the dog was going to make noises wherever he was left. But he finally decided that dog sounds coming from outdoors would be less likely to attract attention than the same sounds from the dormitory upstairs; maybe they'd think it was a neighbor's dog if they heard him barking. Eddie knew he had to replace the clothesline and didn't dare use that again, so he poked around in the shed and found a short length of cord that he could loop around F.G.P.'s neck. He tied the other end to a bush behind the shed.

When he walked away, the dog yelped unhappily. Eddie sighed. He'd known all along that it was silly, what Mr. Caw had said about the dog being a fairy godpuppy. It was only in books that such things happened. This was no more than an ordinary dog, with no more sense than most puppies, who was going to keep barking until he was discovered. Then he'd go to the pound, more than likely, and Eddie would be alone again.

He was surprised, though, at how much he

wanted to keep F.G.P., even if he wasn't magic. He was so soft and warm to touch, and he'd snuggled against Eddie in such a trusting way. If it wasn't for Mrs. Mundy's allergies, would Miss Susan have let him keep a dog?

Well, he thought, climbing the porch steps, maybe Mr. Caw had found someone to take F.G.P. That would be better than sending him to the pound.

He didn't intend to go up the stairs, again; he'd just go on into the dining room where the others would be gathering in a few minutes. He wondered if there was any chance that he could pick up a few crackers to feed F.G.P., if he paused in the kitchen.

Cook was stirring something on the stove. She looked at him and shook her head. "Can't you wait until it's on the table, to see what's to eat?" she asked, but she wasn't cross.

"I'm hungry," Eddie said truthfully. "Could I have an extra piece of toast?"

Mrs. Mundy turned from where she was inspecting something on a big tray. She didn't have to work in the kitchen, but she never thought anyone else could do things right without her supervision, not even Cook. "Nothing's ready yet. You can wait a few more minutes, the same as everyone else," she said.

She dropped slices of bread into the toaster and pushed down the handle, and Cook took her spoon out of the cereal and made a face. "That big toaster isn't working right," she warned. "It won't pop up by itself. You have to watch it or it burns."

"No, you don't," Eddie said. "I fixed it."

"I've told you and told you, Eddie, to leave things alone," Mrs. Mundy snapped. And then she jumped backward and nearly stepped on him because all of a sudden the six slices of bread were catapulted into the air.

One of them landed in the kettle of cereal on the stove; one went down the front of Mrs. Mundy's apron, and the rest fell on the floor.

"I guess I must have got too much spring in it," Eddie said. He would have offered to adjust it, but he decided the way they were shrieking and jumping around, maybe he'd better wait until later.

They weren't paying any attention to him for a few seconds, so he scooped up the toast from the floor and went outside before they could stop him.

Mr. Caw was unloading his pickup, spreading the canvas tarp on the grass again. He looked at Eddie with interest. "Sounds like you've got them going again," he said. "What did you do this time?"

"Nothing to make a fuss about," Eddie said. He stopped to catch his breath. "The toast flies out too far, but I can fix it. I didn't have any bread to test it with, before."

"The dog behave himself during the night? Didn't bark his head off so they called the police or anything like that? Where is he, out in the shed?"

"Tied behind it," Eddie said, not explaining that F.G.P. had spent the night in Eddie's own bed. "I have to feed him the toast now. Excuse me."

F.G.P. was happy to get the toast, even without butter or anything on it. What he wanted most, however, was for Eddie to untie him and play with him.

"I can't," Eddie said. "I have to go eat, or they'll wonder. I'll see if I can get you something better from breakfast."

There wasn't much he could use, though, Eddie thought when they'd taken their places around the table. The broccoli had gotten all squashed last night in Jonas's pockets, and it would be even worse to try to carry oatmeal. There was half an orange at each place, but Eddie didn't think dogs usually ate oranges.

"What're we going to feed him?" Jonas whispered, leaning toward him. "Toast? That's about all we can carry outside."

Arnie heard the whisper. "I'm not giving him *my* toast," he said. "I'd be hungry myself."

Eddie didn't say anything to that. It was true, they'd all be hungry if they gave their food to the dog. Was there any way he could slip into the kitchen, after Cook had done the dishes and gone to market the way she usually did, to find something more?

He spooned brown sugar over his oatmeal and began to eat, not touching his toast. He had to take *something* with him when he went out to F.G.P. It was too bad, too, because the jam this morning was strawberry, his favorite.

Arnie picked up the little packet of jam and looked at it. "When I get home, I'm going to eat a whole jar of jam, all by myself. Why don't they buy jars of jam in this place, instead of these little packages with just enough for one slice of bread?"

"It's cheaper to let us have only a little bit,"

Jonas said. He glanced to see if Mrs Mundy or Miss Susan was looking in his direction from their own table, then put another heaping spoonful of sugar on his cereal. "This way, we don't get any seconds."

Eddie had an idea. "I'll trade my jam for somebody's toast," he said.

Arnie made a strangled sound. "What good's the jam, if there's nothing to put it on?"

"I'll trade it for half a slice of toast. You'll still have some toast, and lots of jam on it."

"Me, too," Jonas said quickly. "I'll give my jam for half a slice of somebody's toast."

"What's all the whispering about?" Jenny wanted to know. The girls usually sat at one end of the table, the boys at the other, and most of the time it was the girls who whispered and shared secrets.

"Nothing you need to know about," Arnie said rudely. He turned to Eddie. "OK. I'll trade you half a slice of toast for your jam."

"I'll trade Jonas for mine," Cary put in. "Here, Jonas."

He'd never have done it that way if he'd known Mrs. Mundy was behind him. Sometimes she got up from the adults' table to get something, and this time she was walking past just as Eddie took the two packets of jam and slid them across the table toward the other boys.

He didn't mean to push them hard enough to go off the edge, and he expected that Arnie would put out a hand to catch them. Only Arnie was startled when Mrs. Mundy suddenly loomed over him, and he didn't do anything at all.

The two little packets of jam skidded past Arnie and onto the floor. Eddie looked down just in time to see those big white shoes come down on top of them.

There was an odd squishing sound, and the plastic containers split. The next thing Eddie saw was the strawberry jam oozing all over the floor and across one of the white shoes in a red smear.

It was, as Jonas said later, as if the jam had been shot out of a gun. Who would have believed that two such tiny packets of jam could make so much of a mess?

Mrs. Mundy looked down at her feet, and her face began to turn color. It got redder and redder, and Eddie wondered if she were going to explode, just like the plastic jam packets.

Eddie lifted horrified eyes to the woman

standing over him. "I didn't mean to . . .I was only trying to—" He stopped. He could tell it wasn't doing any good. Mrs. Mundy looked as if she'd like to hit him.

Luckily Miss Susan rose and came to see what she could do to help. She took one look at the sticky red stuff and spoke calmly. "Mrs. Mundy, why don't you go clean off your shoes and stockings, and the boys will help me wipe up what's on the floor. Cook, could we have some more jam for the boys who lost theirs, please?"

It wasn't the best breakfast time Eddie had ever had. He was glad to escape with Jonas as soon as they'd eaten. They didn't make it out of the dining room, however, before Mrs. Mundy returned, and her voice was angry when she spoke to them all.

"Cook tells me," she said, and it seemed to Eddie that she looked directly at him, "that someone has stolen the clothesline with all my underclothes on it! You are excused, but someone had better return that rope and the clothes before this day is over, if they know what's good for them."

"Let's get out of here," Jonas said under his

breath, and they fled to the yard. Eddie didn't know what all the fuss was about. He hadn't stolen the rope, he'd only borrowed it; and why would anybody get excited about clean underwear at breakfast time? It was perfectly safe, folded under the back steps on top of his book to keep it from getting dirty. The tricky part was going to be to put it all back without anyone seeing him.

Mr. Caw was painting, but he stopped when he saw them and waved a hand at the house. "You young fellows know anything about that? Where my fresh paint is scraped off the side of the house?"

Eddie had forgotten about that damage. He swallowed, wondering what he could say that would help. He couldn't tell if Mr. Caw was really angry or not.

Jonas hadn't thought of anything to say, either. They stood there, dumbly, and Mr. Caw scratched his head. "Looks as if somebody hauled something to that window up there," he told them. "Something that bumped against the paint and scraped it. Like a bucket, maybe. With a dog in it?"

Eddie swallowed again and made his voice

work. He didn't want Mr. Caw to be mad at him. "We didn't mean to do it. We didn't know the bucket would hit the house. Maybe I could climb up your ladder and fix it?"

"I think I'd better fix it myself," Mr. Caw decided. "Is the dog up there now?"

Eddie shook his head. "No, he's tied out behind the shed."

"You better keep him there, or somewhere out of sight," Mr. Caw suggested. "I didn't find anybody to keep him until you get out of here, but maybe if I took him home my wife might agree to have him for a guest. Just for a while."

The thought of losing F.G.P. when he'd had him such a short time was painful, but Eddie could see the sense of it. Especially if he wasn't a real fairy godpuppy, and he kept on causing problems.

He hadn't stopped causing problems yet, because in the silence they heard him whining, and then he began to bark. He barked and barked, until it was a miracle Mrs. Mundy didn't come out looking for him.

"Excuse me," Eddie said. "I'd better go."

He and Jonas were halfway to the shed when Barry ran toward them from the house.

"You're going to have to find a way to keep him quiet," he said. "Mrs. Mundy is sneezing, and she says there's a dog around somewhere, she's heard him."

"She couldn't be sneezing because of F.G.P.," Eddie protested. "He isn't anywhere near her."

"She says it makes her nose itch just to know there's a dog in the neighborhood." Barry shrugged. "I think it's crazy, too, but that's what she says."

"The only thing that keeps him quiet is for somebody to stay with him," Jonas pointed out. "Maybe we'll have to take turns doing that."

"Mr. Linders is coming today to cut the grass," Barry warned. "So you'll have to move him. If Mr. Linders sees him, he'll report to Mrs. Mundy for sure."

They exchanged glances. "We better take him back to the dormitory," Jonas said finally. "We can take turns with him. Maybe some of the other kids will help, too. Is Mr. Caw going to take him home tonight, to see if his wife will keep him for a while?"

Eddie didn't know whether he hoped so or not. "If somebody will be sure Mrs. Mundy's not around, I'll sneak him inside. We can't use the bucket again, I have to put the clothesline back, so I'll have to go up the back stairs if the door's still unlocked."

"It is," Barry said. "I just came out. I'll see if Cook's busy so she won't notice you."

It was hard work, moving F.G.P. around without being seen. By this time the girls knew something interesting was going on, and Jenny and Cheryl caught Eddie before he reached the top of the stairs.

He didn't worry about their telling. They thought F.G.P. was darling, and they talked baby talk to him, which the silly dog seemed to like.

"He's so soft," Jenny said.

"Can I hold him?" Cheryl asked.

"We better wait until he's safe in the dormitory," Eddie decided. "How'd you like to take a turn watching him and keeping him quiet so Mrs. Mundy won't hear him?"

It worked out pretty well, because there were plenty of kids who knew about him, now, and they all wanted to help. Nobody wanted Mrs. Mundy to find him.

Eddie instructed each of them in how to

care for F.G.P., warning them all that the important thing was that he not be allowed to make sounds that would draw adult attention. He went off to attend to fixing the clothesline, thinking the dog would be perfectly safe and happy with the girls playing with him.

So he was shocked to return half an hour later to find both Jenny and Cheryl nearly in tears.

"He got away," Jenny said. "We couldn't catch him, Eddie! He's disappeared!"

FIVE

F.G.P. wasn't in the boys' dormitory. He wasn't in the girls' dormitory. They didn't find him in the boys' bathroom nor in the one the girls used. They peeked into Mrs. Mundy's bathroom and saw no sign that the dog had been there, either.

"Could he have gone downstairs?" Eddie asked. There was an uncomfortable lump in his stomach. Some fairy godpuppy, he thought bitterly. He was too foolish to stay where he'd be safe, and now they were probably all in trouble.

Jonas had come up the stairs behind Eddie. "I didn't see him. He must still be up here somewhere."

"He couldn't have gone down the back way," Jenny pointed out. "That door's closed."

They all looked at one another, and Eddie swallowed hard. "There's only one other place," he said. All eyes turned toward the door of Mrs. Mundy's room.

It was only open a narrow crack. Could a puppy have gone through such a small opening?

Eddie touched the door with his fingertips, pushing it gently inward. "You in there, F.G.P.?" he asked softly.

There was a scurrying sound as the dog's toenails clicked on the polished floor. F.G.P. appeared in the crack, carrying something in his mouth that made Eddie cry out.

"Oh, no! You stupid dog!"

It was a blue slipper, a very large one, that they would have recognized as belonging to Mrs. Mundy even it it hadn't come out of her room. Eddie jerked it out of F.G.P.'s mouth and stared at it in dismay.

The dog had been chewing on it, and there was a hole in the toe big enough for Eddie to put three fingers into.

Now what did he do?

For the second time in two days, Eddie fought not to cry. Mrs. Mundy would never forgive him, never.

F.G.P. looked up at him and wagged his tail. Eddie put out his good hand and shoved the door all the way open; he might as well know the worst, he thought.

The mate to the blue slipper lay on a rug beside the bed,—what was left of it. F.G.P. had chewed it into a raggedy heap. Jenny made a little moaning sound.

Jonas groaned. "I hope Mr. Caw is going to take that dog home with him tonight," he said, "or Mrs. Mundy will make soup out of him."

Cheryl looked at him in horror. "No, she won't!"

"Well, not *really*," Jonas told her. "But it'll be almost that bad. We better hide what's left of the slippers, hadn't we, Eddie? Maybe she'll think she left them somewhere else, and they got lost."

It didn't seem likely that Mrs. Mundy could be so fooled, but Eddie didn't know what else to do. He stuffed the two slippers into the sling, behind his cast, where they made a bunchy lump, and wondered where he could put them so they'd never be found.

The girls took F.G.P. back to the dormitory with the promise that they wouldn't allow him to escape again, even if they had to use a couple of belts to tie him to the leg of a bed. He wouldn't cry, they thought, if they stayed with him and talked to him.

As Eddie went down the stairs, he saw Mrs. Ferris, the woman who helped Miss Susan in the office, talking to Mrs. Jordan, who did most of the cleaning. They both smiled and spoke to him.

"Hello, Eddie."

"Hi, Eddie. I hear you broke your arm again." Mrs. Jordan shook her head. "You're a wild one, all right."

Eddie wished people would stop talking about him, though at least these two weren't cross about it. He hoped they couldn't see any of the blue slippers through the material of his sling, and he walked past them as quickly as he could.

The best place he could think of to dispose of the slippers was in the big plastic bags in which Mr. Linders put the grass clippings. Maybe the old man wouldn't notice that there was something else in with the clippings when he hauled them away.

He and Jonas took their turn tending the puppy after that, but it wasn't much fun any more. Even when F.G.P. licked his chin, Eddie didn't smile, and the warm softness of the small body pressed against him didn't make him feel better. It only made him sad.

Lonnie and Cary took a turn at keeping the

dog while the others had lunch; Mrs. Mundy was lying down with a headache, and Miss Susan wasn't nearly so strict about people coming late to the table. The boys simply explained that they'd been playing and didn't notice what time it was; and she told them to sit down and eat at once, so that Cook could clear things away.

Miss Susan gave Eddie such a loving look when he left the dining room that it made his eyes sting again. At least *she* liked him, and when she mentioned his shortcomings she usually laughed and wasn't ever mean about them.

He supposed he'd have to go upstairs and take over his dog again, but something inside him didn't want to. He didn't want to like F.G.P. too much, because he knew he wasn't going to be able to keep him. He went out the back door and around the house—and came upon the painter.

Mr. Caw was just coming down his ladder; he had repaired the places where the bucket had scraped the fresh paint off the side of the house.

"I can't see why you're so eager to leave here," he said. "This is the most interesting place I ever worked."

Eddie stood there, saying nothing. He was

catching on to Mr. Caw. Mr. Caw said everything with a straight face, even when he was kidding. But Eddie still didn't know what to answer, so he said nothing at all.

"Had a cup of coffee in the kitchen just now," Mr. Caw said. He stepped off the ladder and moved it a few feet, but he didn't climb back up it again. "It seems somebody stole Mrs. Mundy's underwear last night and the clothesline along with it. This morning the clothesline is back, with a section of bicycle chain replacing one end of it, and the clothes are all there except one stocking, which oddly enough was caught on a rose bush. Full of runs."

When Eddie remained silent, Mr. Caw went on. "Mrs. Mundy's missing her good blue slippers. And somebody cleaned out the creamed chipped beef Cook had left in the refrigerator. Why would anybody want cold chipped beef?" He put down one pail and picked up another one, stirring its contents with a stick. "I heard the boys had an awful time settling down last night after they'd gone to bed. Giggled and whispered and made noises like a dog."

He looked keenly at Eddie. "Something going on all the time, isn't there?"

"You made it all up," Eddie accused around

the painful lump in his throat. He was begin-ning to think that Mr. Caw wasn't very funny. "There isn't any such thing as a fairy godpuppy, and I'm in all kinds of trouble because of him. He's a pretty good dog, but he's not magic. He's not even very smart."

Mr. Caw made a queer noise, deep in his throat. "That so? I'd have sworn he was magic, the way he turned up. You're sure, are you?"

Again the tears stung in Eddie's eyes, but he didn't let them escape. "I have to figure out some way to get Mrs. Mundy a new pair of slip-pers," he said.

"The dog did that, did he?" Mr. Caw hesi-tated. "Well, I tell you, boy, I didn't mean to mislead you or get you into trouble. I guess it's my fault as much as yours. I tell you what." He reached into his back pocket and got out his wallet. "I think the slippers are my responsibil-ity. Here, you buy her another pair, all right?"

Eddie took the money and put it into his sling, under the cast where it wouldn't be no-ticed. "It wasn't a very funny joke, Mr. Caw. Making me hope . . . something that couldn't happen."

"I can see that," Mr. Caw said. "But even if you're no beauty, Eddie, you're tough, aren't you? You aren't going to give up, are you, just because that dog isn't really magic?"

"Nobody'll adopt me," Eddie reminded him. "Nobody wants me."

Mr. Caw fished in a pocket for a package of gum and pulled out a stick for himself and one for Eddie. "Then you've got a real job ahead of you. You've got to decide who's the most important person to please and *make* her like you."

For a minute Eddie thought Mr. Caw was crazy. He'd been trying to make Mrs. Mundy like him ever since he'd come to this place, and it never did any good. He did everything wrong.

And then, watching Mr. Caw climb the ladder and begin to swish the brush in neat strokes across the boards, Eddie had an idea. He'd forget about Mrs. Mundy. He'd try to please someone who could really help him, someone who might take him out of the Riverside Children's Home.

He'd work on Mr. Caw.

That evening Mr. Caw told Eddie to bring F.G.P. down to him, and he'd take him home. "Surprise my wife," he said. "At least at my house he won't get you into any more trouble."

Eddie brought the puppy down after every-

one else had gone to the dining room, while Jonas watched to make sure it was safe. He put F.G.P. into the seat of the pickup, stroking the soft brown head, then quickly closed the door. F.G.P. stood up on his hind legs and looked out the window, scratching at the glass.

"Guess he got sort of fond of you," Mr. Caw said. "You liked him pretty well, too, didn't you?"

"Yes," Eddie admitted. It felt as if the tears were stuck in his throat, worse than the ones in his eyes.

Mr. Caw nodded. "Well, I'll take good care of him."

After he'd loaded up the truck and driven away, Eddie had to go off to the apple tree by himself for a while before he dared to be where anyone could see him.

Miss Susan came out to meet him when he headed back for the house. "I know you like that tree, Eddie, but it's really beyond bounds, you know. It would be better if you set a good example for the others and stayed inside the fence."

The way he was feeling, Eddie didn't think it mattered. "OK," he agreed.

Miss Susan put an arm around him, giving him a little hug. She smelled nice, and her silky dress was soft against his cheek, but he didn't want the other kids to see her hugging him. Especially Arnie. He pulled away before they reached the house.

That night in bed he allowed some of the tears to trickle silently down his cheeks, and one of them ran into his ear. It might have been funny, Eddie thought, if it hadn't been so sad.

SIX

Mr. Caw reported that F.G.P. was getting along all right with Mrs. Caw, though she'd given her husband one of those special looks that meant she wasn't exactly pleased with what he'd done.

"She'll be good to him," Mr. Caw said. "We always had dogs when our boys were growing up."

Eddie's heart beat a little faster. "Do you have children, then?"

"Oh, they're men, now. One lives in Chicago, and the other lives in California."

"Oh. So there's just you and Mrs. Caw. Do you have a house of your own?"

Mr. Caw always kept working while he talked to Eddie. Otherwise, he said, he'd never get anything done. "Why, certainly. I've got a little place with a yard and a garden. Mostly flowers, my wife likes flowers."

"Is she nice?" Eddie asked.

"Grace? Oh, yes, she's pretty reasonable for

a woman," Mr. Caw said, mounting the ladder. "Hand me up that other brush, will you?"

It took Mr. Caw a couple of days to catch onto the fact that he was being worked on. Instead of playing with the other kids or reading so much, Eddie hung around the painter. He sort of liked watching the paint go on so smoothly, covering up the old wood. It would be a neat job to have, he thought, if you didn't have to paint things such stupid colors.

Eddie stirred paint and carried the buckets when the ladder was moved and cleaned the brushes. He brought Mr. Caw his lunch from the truck so he could eat in the shade. He helped move the big canvas tarp that kept the paint from getting all over the grass. Mrs. Mundy was very particular about the grass, and she was all upset when Eddie walked in some paint and tracked it onto the porch, leaving ghostly looking tan footprints.

For the most part, Eddie thought he was being a big help, until he backed into the ladder and overturned it into an open can of paint. Mr. Caw didn't yell at him, though, the way almost everybody else would have.

Once they'd cleaned up the spilled paint from the tarp, Eddie decided he'd better try to sound Mr. Caw out a little. "Aren't you lonely with your sons living so far away?" he asked.

"Oh, they write home, and call on special days . . ." His voice trailed off and Mr. Caw looked at Eddie suspiciously.

Eddie kicked at the corner of the tarp to show that what he was talking about wasn't important, though of course it was.

"Doesn't your wife get lonely?" he asked.

"Boy," said Mr. Caw, "I have the feeling you're leading up to something."

"Who, me?" Eddie held his eyes wide open, the way people did in the movies when they wanted someone to think they were innocent. "I'm just interested, Mr. Caw."

Mr. Caw sniffed and didn't say any more, but he watched Eddie out of the corner of his eye for a while after that.

Eddie had thought Mr. Caw might be easier to get around, and it worried him that the painter wasn't falling easily into the plan. Maybe, he thought unhappily, he'd better work on Mrs. Mundy, too. In case anybody ever came who wanted a boy and who wouldn't mind stiff red hair and freckles if she told them he was a *nice* boy.

When Mrs. Mundy came home during the

afternoon, her arms full of packages, Eddie ran to meet her.

"Can I carry something for you, Mrs. Mundy?"

She looked at him the way she always looked at Eddie, as if he didn't smell very good.

"Well, maybe this sack," she said finally. "It's slipping. Be careful, it's breakable."

Eddie meant to be careful. He tried hard. But the sack was so big that when he held it against his chest with his good arm, he couldn't see over it. He didn't see the hose stretched across the sidewalk, so he could hardly help what happened.

Eddie and the sack went sprawling; cans rolled out across the grass, and the sack ripped down the side so nobody could even pick it up again. One egg broke in a gooey mess over his shoe.

Mrs. Mundy shook her head. "I knew you couldn't be trusted to carry anything without dropping it. Go in and get another bag, then pick everything up."

Eddie scrambled to his feet. "Yes, ma'am," he told her. "I'll clean it all up, right away." When he'd finished the job and taken every-

thing in to Cook, Eddie kicked at the hose as he spoke to Mr. Caw. "I couldn't please Mrs. Mundy if I tried all my life," he said.

"Don't know but what you're right about that one," Mr. Caw muttered, going back to his painting. "Another couple of days, and I'll be done here. Come on, boy, bring that other pail and let's get on with it."

Eddie tugged at the pail until he had it where Mr. Caw wanted it. When the painter had gone, he wouldn't even get a report on how F.G.P. was doing, he thought sadly. "You'll take good care of F.G.P., won't you?" he asked. "He needs someone understanding. Someone who'll make allowances for him being so young, you know."

He didn't know what to make of the look that Mr. Caw gave him then, a strange, long look.

Miss Susan was in her office, and she looked up and smiled when Eddie peered in. "Hi, Eddie. What are you up to?"

"I need to go to town," Eddie said. "I have to buy something. Is it all right?"

He held his breath, afraid that she'd asked

what it was, and worse yet, where he'd gotten the money to spend. She didn't, though.

"We don't usually allow the children to go all the way downtown," she said. "I'd rather none of you went on the bus alone."

"I don't need to go on the bus. I can walk. Six blocks," he told her. There was a shoe store in a small shopping center on the edge of town. He thought he could buy slippers, there.

"Oh. Well, I suppose you could do that. Be back in time for supper, though. Maybe it would be a good idea if someone went with you. How about Jonas?"

"OK. I'll ask him," Eddie agreed. "Thanks, Miss Susan."

Jonas was perfectly willing to stop wrestling with Dick and Arnie to go with him. Mr. Caw called down to Eddie as they came around the corner of the house. "I asked Miss Susan if you could come to my house for supper tomorrow," he told Eddie. "I thought maybe you'd like to visit that fool dog."

"Yes, sir, I would," Eddie said. "I'd like to meet your wife, too."

He wasn't sure he should have said that last part about Mrs. Caw, because Mr. Caw looked funny again. It was too late to worry about it now, though, since he'd already said it.

"You be ready," Mr. Caw said, "when it's time for me to go home, all right?" and Eddie agreed at once.

The boys walked the six blocks as fast as they could, feeling quite grown up at being allowed to go by themselves. On the way, Eddie explained to Jonas what he had in mind. "Maybe, if his wife likes me, they'll adopt me. Or at least be foster parents. And then I could have F.G.P., too."

"I hope so," Jonas told him. "My friends the Castles are coming on Sunday, and I'm going to go home with them. Miss Susan said I could stay a week. Maybe," he added hopefully, "they'll want me to stay longer. Maybe I can go and live with them."

"I'll miss you, but I hope you get to live with them. Look, Jonas, there's the shoe store, and that says SALE, doesn't it?"

The man inside the store looked at them over his glasses. "The toy store's next door," he said.

"We don't want toys," Eddie told him. "We need to buy some bedroom slippers. Blue ones."

"Oh, that's different. What size?"

Eddie looked at Jonas. Jonas looked at Eddie. They hadn't the faintest idea what size Mrs. Mundy wore.

"Big," Eddie said. "Like those, on that table."

"This pair? Yes, these are a bargain. On sale at half price. But we'd have to know the size. For your mother, are they?"

"No," Eddie said. "Just for a . . . a lady. How do you tell what size?"

"It might be wise to ask the lady," the clerk suggested.

"No, I can't do that. Isn't there any other way?"

"Oh, a surprise, eh? Well, if you could get hold of a pair of her shoes and get me the numbers on the inside of them . . ."

Numbers inside? Eddie scowled, trying to remember. Had there been numbers inside the slippers F.G.P. had chewed?

His brow cleared. "Ten," he said. "There was number 10."

"You sure about that? Ten is rather large for a lady."

"Don't you have any that big?" Eddie asked anxiously.

"Oh, yes. I think I have one pair that size

on the sale table. When you buy shoes on sale, you can't bring them back, you know. So you'd better not buy them unless you're sure about the size. These aren't blue, though. They're green."

He brought out the slippers, large, wide ones, much prettier than the ones F.G.P. had destroyed.

"These are all right," Eddie decided. "She has big feet. I know there was a number 10 in the old ones, just like these."

So the slippers were wrapped up, and Eddie paid for them. When they went out into the street, he still had some money left.

They stopped in front of the toy store window, looking at toy guns and color books and puzzles and cars and trucks and dolls. His money would buy a lot of things, and Mr. Caw hadn't said he wanted the change returned to him.

Then Eddie remembered that he was going to meet Mrs. Caw tomorrow. He remembered what Mr. Caw had said. He had to decide who was important and make her like him.

Hope rose in his chest. There was a chance, just a chance, that he could please Mrs. Caw. It had been his experience (viewed strictly from the sidelines) that it was the ladies who decided which child to take; probably it was the ladies who decided whether or not they wanted a child at all. Mrs. Caw had two sons, so she must have liked boys at one time; maybe she still did.

He would be on his best behavior when he visited her, of course. But wouldn't it help if he took her a present, too?

"We're closing in fifteen minutes," the girl said when they went into the dime store. Eddie nodded and walked quickly down the aisle, looking for the right thing for a present for Mrs. Caw.

He found it, the perfect gift, in time to pay for it before the store closed. Jonas agreed with him. Surely such a fine present would win Mrs. Caw over if anything would.

It was late, and they had to run part of the way home. Miss Susan laughed and said, "Hurry, or you'll be late!" but she sounded so pleasant that Eddie didn't really worry.

Upstairs, he unwrapped the green slippers and took them into Mrs. Mundy's bedroom. He was placing them on the rug beside her bed when the door swung inward.

Eddie held his breath, knowing Mrs. Mundy would never believe, no matter what the evidence, that he wasn't up to mischief.

But it wasn't Mrs. Mundy. Miss Susan peeked around the edge of the door. "Eddie, what are you doing in here?"

Then she saw the slippers. "Oh, I see. They're lovely, Eddie. Hurry, though, the others have gone in to supper, and there's strawberry shortcake tonight. Everyone's eager to eat."

They ran downstairs together, arriving breathless in the dining room after everyone else was already sitting down. Mrs. Mundy didn't speak to him, but Eddie know by the look on her face that she would have, if Miss Susan hadn't been late with him. He'd try to be on time for meals for the next few days, he thought.

The girls were whispering among themselves, and after a moment or two Eddie realized they were talking excitedly about Miss Susan.

"What's going on?" he wanted to know.

Jenny looked at the other girls. "I told you, boys never notice anything important. It's Miss Susan's ring. I suppose you didn't even see it!"

The boys exchanged glances. Arnie shrugged. "What're you talking about?"

"Her *engagement ring,* of course! It's a diamond ring, and that's why she's looking so happy! She's going to get married!"

Eddie felt a sinking sensation in his stomach. He glanced over to where Miss Susan was talking to Mrs. Ferris, and she *did* look very happy and excited.

"Is she going to keep on working here?" Eddie asked, his voice sounding hollow.

"Nobody knows yet," Cheryl told him. "We all hope so. At least while we're all still here."

Eddie thought miserably that he'd probably be here forever. Having Miss Susan here too was the only thing that made living in the Riverside Children's Home bearable. What would he do if she went away?

It wouldn't matter so much to the others, since they'd all be going on to real homes before long anyway. If anything, he thought, that silly dog had brought him bad luck rather than good. He wished he'd never met Mr. Caw, never heard of such a thing as a fairy godpuppy.

With his luck, Eddie thought, Mrs. Caw wouldn't like him, either. It probably wasn't even worthwhile to go and meet her.

He knew he couldn't go to sleep with this

hanging over his head, that Miss Susan might be leaving soon when she got married. When the other kids scattered after supper, Eddie gathered all the courage he had and hurried to catch Miss Susan before she left for home.

SEVEN

"Miss Susan! Wait!" Eddie called.

She turned, ready to get into her car and drive away, and Eddie ran toward her. "I'm running late, Eddie. Can it wait until tomorrow?"

It couldn't. He'd never sleep until he knew whether she was going to go away or not. His breath came in little gasps because he had run so hard.

"They said you're getting married," he said, looking into her face. "That you're engaged."

Her smile was the same as always. "Yes. That's right. We're going to be married here at the home, because you children are the nearest thing I have to a family, and I want you all to be part of the wedding. In fact, I want *you* to be the ring bearer. Do you know what that is?"

He had to know the worst. "Are you going to keep on working here, after you're married?"

Her expression changed. "No, Eddie, I'm not. When Patrick and I are married, we're going to move away, to where Patrick works. Don't worry, though, you'll be well taken care of, I promise."

"Soon?" he asked. "Are you going soon?"

"We'll be married in two weeks," Miss Susan said gently. "Eddie—"

But he didn't wait to hear the rest. It was more than he could bear, to know that she was leaving him, the only one who had really cared for him since his grandmother had died. He ran away faster than he'd ever run before, which was awkward with his arm in a cast.

Though she called after him, he didn't stop. He ran into the house and up the stairs and into the empty dormitory, where he flung himself on the bed and buried his face in the pillow.

He stayed there for a long time. It was almost dark when he finally got up and washed his face by splashing water over it. Some of the water got on the cast and he wiped it off, because he knew that if it got too wet it would get soft and fall apart, and then he'd have to have another cast put on it. He knew that, because when he'd broken his other arm, the first time, he'd taken a shower with the cast on and everyone had been quite annoyed with him.

He went slowly downstairs to where the voices were. Some of the kids were playing Monopoly and a few more were watching TV. Mrs. Mundy was talking to Cook, who must have stayed late for some reason.

"I can't imagine where they came from," Mrs. Mundy said, and for once she didn't sound cross at all. "Beautiful slippers, they are, and they feel so good! My feet hurt all the time, you know, but in these slippers they're much better. I'm tempted to wear them downstairs during the daytime, they feel so good."

"Makes a person irritable, to have feet that hurt," Cook said. She began to move toward the door.

Eddie paused on the stairs, not wanting to attract their attention.

Mrs. Mundy frowned slightly. "Why, do you think I'm irritable?"

"Well," Cook told her, "when your feet are the worst I notice you're crabby with the kids. Especially that little Eddie. I don't think he means any harm."

Mrs. Mundy sighed. "That one's a problem, all right. It's hard not to get cross with someone who's always in trouble. Well, I guess you want to catch your bus. Good night. I'll see you in the morning."

When Cook had gone, Mrs. Mundy, wearing the new green slippers, went into the living room. "Time to be putting the games away," she said, "and getting ready for bed."

Eddie didn't want to see any of them. Yet they'd notice if he wasn't there when the others went to bed. He wondered if the police would come after him if he ran away.

Then he remembered that tomorrow he was supposed to visit Mr. and Mrs. Caw. He remembered that he had a present to take to the painter's wife, and that there was just a chance he might be able to make her like him.

He turned around and went back up the stairs; by the time the others came, he was in bed with his eyes closed, pretending to be asleep.

Eddie was ready ahead of time, waiting for Mr. Caw to pack up his paint pails and his tarp and his ladders for the last time. He had finished painting, and he wouldn't be coming back. Jonas was leaving tomorrow, and in two weeks Miss Susan would be gone. It had been a terrible day, Eddie thought; and he hoped that it wouldn't get any worse.

That morning at breakfast all the children had known that someone was coming that day to choose a child. No one could say how they knew, because Mrs. Mundy and Miss Susan never told them ahead of time, but they always knew. Perhaps it was the extra waxing and polishing that was done in the front hall, or the fresh flowers put in Miss Susan's office (where they wouldn't set off Mrs. Mundy's allergies) or the fact that Mrs. Mundy wore her best dress.

Eddie had known, along with the others, that today was the important day for *someone*. He tried to tell himself that there was no use in hoping that the lucky one would be *him*. It was hard not to wonder, though, if Mrs. Mundy was happy enough when her feet didn't hurt so that she would be more kind in what she said about him.

Usually the children went out in the back to play after they'd made their beds, but on a day when visitors were coming they all managed to find something to do at the front of the building.

Eddie had watched as Mr. Caw painted the last of the trim around the front porch. The painter paused to look at him.

"What's all the excitement?"

"Someone is coming to pick out a child," Eddie told him. "To take home with them."

He knew that wasn't really the way it worked. The people would already have been told about the child they were interested in and seen a picture. Miss Susan had talked to them and they'd been approved as adoptive parents, and now they would meet the child they had chosen. He always felt, however, as if they *might* change their minds and choose him, instead.

And then he heard the car and forgot about Mr. Caw. It was a big pale blue car, the prettiest one Eddie had ever see, and the couple who got out of it were attractive, too. The man was big and tall, and the lady wore a pink dress and a flowery hat.

As they came up the walk, the lady looked right at Eddie and smiled. He felt his heart leap in his chest. What would it be like to have such a pretty lady for a mother, to make cookies for you and put bandages on your skinned knees?

"My goodness," the lady said, looking at Eddie's cast, "what happened to you?"

His throat was so dry he could hardly speak. "I fell out of a tree," he said. He liked her soft voice and her smile.

Mrs. Mundy came out of the house behind

him, huge in her green flowered dress, and as she spoke Eddie knew he had lost again.

"He's always falling off something," she told the lady. "That's the third cast he's had in six months. Never saw such a boy for getting into trouble. Please come inside, Mrs. Graham, Mr. Graham. The little girl you wanted to see will be right down."

They walked on into the house without a backward glance. Eddie bit down on his lower lip and walked closer to Mr. Caw. The painter was ready to move his ladder, and Eddie helped him silently. Mr. Caw got out a stick of gum and offered Eddie a stick.

"People didn't look so good, eh?"

"They looked fine," Eddie said quietly. "The lady asked me about my cast."

"That was a good start. Wasn't it?"

"Would have been," Eddie said. "Only Mrs. Mundy came along and told them I was always getting into trouble. I guess nobody wants a boy who's always getting into trouble."

Eddie didn't quite understand what Mr. Caw muttered, and Mr. Caw didn't repeat it, but it sounded like, "Didn't know there was any other kind."

And now it was time to go and visit Mrs. Caw. Mrs. Mundy had checked to make sure he'd washed behind his ears, and he hoped that the red would have gone out of the ear she'd taken hold of before he got to the Caws' house.

Miss Susan came out onto the steps beside him. "You look nice, Eddie," she said cheerfully. "I'm sure you and Mrs. Caw are going to get along fine. What's in the carton?"

"A present for Mrs. Caw," Eddie said. He lifted the lid so she could see into the little white box. "Do you think she'll like it?"

"I don't see how she could help it. Have a good time, Eddie, and tomorrow you can tell me all about the visit, all right?"

"Tomorrow's Sunday," Eddie reminded her. "You don't come on Sundays."

"I will tomorrow, to talk to the Castles when they come for Jonas," Miss Susan told him. "Have fun, Eddie."

He was afraid he wasn't going to have fun at all. He felt strange, riding beside Mr. Caw in the truck, scrubbed and combed and wearing his best clothes. The present in the carton between his knees now seemed a stupid one, and he decided that after today was over, maybe he'd run away.

He had no idea where he would go or what he would do. But anything seemed better than staying on at the Riverside Children's Home without Miss Susan and without even Jonas or Mr. Caw.

It wasn't very far. Eddie stared at the small house with the fresh white paint and green shutters. There was a yard enclosed by a white picket fence, with lots of trees and flowers.

Mr. Caw honked the horn as he parked in the driveway, and a woman came out onto the front steps.

Eddie had been a little bit afraid that she might be like Mrs. Mundy, hurried and hurrying, frowning when anyone interrupted her routine, cross when anybody did anything wrong.

To his relief, Mrs. Caw didn't look at all like Mrs. Mundy. She wasn't as young as the lady in the pink dress and flowered hat, but she had kind blue eyes and she held out a hand to Eddie.

"Hello, Eddie. I've been hearing such things about you!"

Eddie cast an alarmed and reproachful glance at Mr. Caw, who was looking in the mailbox and didn't seem to notice.

"Come on inside. You'll want to see F.G.P.

He's in the kitchen, eating. He has a hard name to say, for an old tongue like mine."

Eddie wondered how her tongue could be older than the rest of her, but it didn't seem polite to ask. He went with her into the house. It was a comfortable place, with carpets and soft chairs and pictures. There was bright tile on the kitchen floor, and F.G.P. was standing with both front feet in his dish so that the dog food had spilled out.

"He's rather messy," said Mrs. Caw. "He needs someone to teach him. So far neither of us has had much time for that kind of thing."

"He's very young you know," Eddie told her earnestly. He hoped she didn't mean to send F.G.P. to the pound because he was messy. "He'll learn."

At the sound of Eddie's voice, the dog came flying across the room. He leaped up and licked happily at Eddie's face.

"He cries at night," Mrs. Caw said. "I wonder if he was used to sleeping with someone?"

"I think so." Eddie's tone was guarded. He knew lots of grownups didn't approve of dogs in beds.

"You might give him a run in the back yard

while I finish up supper," Mrs. Caw suggested. "Through that door, there."

Eddie was glad to have a few minutes alone with F.G.P. He had missed him more than he'd have thought possible to miss a silly little animal that had slept with him for only one night.

It was plain that F.G.P. had missed him, too. They raced around the back yard with the puppy yelping in excitement and getting under Eddie's feet until he went sprawling. He didn't feel like laughing, though. Not when he knew he'd have to go back to the home soon, and F.G.P. would have to stay here.

Mrs. Caw was a good cook, and she hadn't made anything that Eddie disliked. All the vegetables were raw, the way he liked them, and nobody seemed to care how much catsup he put on his hamburger. Butter melted in a golden pool on his mashed potatoes; and when Mrs. Caw brought out the dessert, Eddie hoped he'd left enough room for it. The chocolate cake was thick and rich and covered with dark frosting that melted on his tongue.

And then, just when he thought the evening was going very well for once, Eddie put out his hand and knocked over his glass of milk.

It ran in little rivers and lakes on the table-cloth, and the glass rolled over the edge of the table and smashed on the floor.

Eddie stared, stricken, at the mess. When he could make his mouth work, he whispered, "I'm sorry. I'll clean it up."

When he dared to look at Mrs. Caw, though, she wasn't angry. "All right," she agreed. "Take these paper towels. I'll clean up the table, and you get the floor. Be careful of the glass, now, that you don't cut yourself. F.G.P., you get your nose out of there before you get hurt!"

Eddie cleaned up the glass and then the spilled milk from the red tile, his heart sinking. He'd almost been having a good time, and now he'd gone and spoiled everything. Even if Mrs. Caw was being polite because he was a guest, Eddie knew women didn't like boys who spilled and broke things.

After supper he went out into the yard again with F.G.P., but it wasn't much fun. He might just as well go back to the home right now, he thought.

He was glad when Mr. Caw told him it was time to go.

"Thank you for supper," he told Mrs. Caw in a low voice. "It was very good."

"I'm glad you could come and visit that poor lonesome dog," Mrs. Caw said, sounding surprisingly cheerful. "After all those stories I heard, I thought we'd have more than one small accident. That's pretty good, I think, for a boy who breaks arms and legs all over the place when he's home."

Eddie looked sadly at Mr. Caw. He had told her, then, and Eddie had never really had any chance to win her over, even at the beginning. And then he remembered the present, which he'd set down on a little table when F.G.P. came running to greet him. It wouldn't do any good now, but he might as well give it to Mrs. Caw, anyway. He was sure Mrs. Mundy would never let him keep it himself.

He went and got the carton and put it into Mrs. Caw's hand.

"It's a present. I forgot it," Eddie mumbled.

"A present! My goodness." Mrs. Caw sounded pleased. She looked into the paper carton. "A turtle! Gracious, I haven't had a turtle since old Shorty!"

"Did you have a turtle before? Do you know what to feed him?"

"Oh, yes, one of my boys gave me a turtle one year for my birthday. He didn't like turtle food, so we had to dig worms for him in the garden."

Eddie nodded, satisfied. Mrs. Caw would take good care of the turtle.

"Thank you, Eddie. This was very thoughtful of you. Now you'll have two friends to come and visit once in a while, F.G.P. and the turtle. You'll have to help me think of a name for him."

Once in a while, she'd said. She had no intention of adopting him, or even being a foster parent. They'd only invited him to visit.

"You remind me so much of my own boys," Mrs. Caw told him. "Falling out of trees and bringing home animals and eating more than a grown man. It makes me sorry I'm not younger. It takes a young woman to keep up with youngsters, except in short visits. But we'll invite you again, Eddie, so you play with F.G.P. and see how the turtle's doing. All right?"

"All right," Eddie said. He could hardly wait to get into the truck and leave, because she'd told him plain enough that what he'd guessed was true. The Caws didn't want him as part of their family. Nobody did.

Mr. Caw tried to carry on a conversation as he drove back to the home, but Eddie didn't feel like talking. He supposed there was no way he could get F.G.P. to go with him when he ran away; he'd never find the Caws house by himself, and it was too far to walk to, anyway.

There was nobody to talk to when he reached the dormitory. Jonas was packing for his trip with the Castle family, and Arnie was teasing the younger boys, and nobody paid any attention to Eddie.

It was just like always, Eddie thought. Probably the way it would always be.

EIGHT

The Castles were a jolly black family. They came in a big station wagon and loaded Jonas's suitcase in the back with the smaller children and drove away, with hands waving goodbye out every window.

Eddie was happy for Jonas, but lonely for himself. He wished Miss Susan hadn't asked him not to go to the apple tree outside the fence, because he wanted very much to sit there in the thick branches where no one could see him.

He'd have to find another place, one where no one would disturb him. Not that anybody paid any attention to him, wherever he went. The girls were talking about Miss Susan's wedding, and the boys were building a fort out of cardboard boxes and some old lumber Mr. Linders hadn't yet hauled away after he tore down a small storage shed. If he hadn't been so depressed, Eddie would have joined them. But Arnie was bossing everybody around, telling them what to do and how to do it, and Eddie wasn't in the mood for that.

Arnie taunted him as Eddie walked away. "Eddie, Eddie, go to beddy! Don't forget to take your teddy!"

Eddie ignored him. He didn't feel up to making a stupid rhyme to answer back, and Miss Susan had once told him that the best way to respond to a tormentor was not to respond at all but to walk away.

The trouble was, there weren't many places to walk away *to*. Not without leaving the grounds, which he wasn't supposed to do. Unless, of course, he ran away altogether.

He kept thinking about that. He didn't know anywhere to go, and he didn't have any money. Maybe if he saved up a supply of food that he could carry with him, it would keep him from starving until he found a place to stay where they'd let him work for his meals.

It took his mind off how lonesome he was, to plan that way. He went around to the back of the house, but the door was locked. Cook must already have gone out.

He could get in the front way, though, Eddie decided. He took the long way around the house so he wouldn't pass the boys who were building the cardboard fort again.

To his surprise, he saw Mr. Caw's pickup parked in front of the building, right behind Miss Susan's car. And he heard their voices on the front porch, almost over his head. Eddie ducked into an azalea bush and listened.

"I like the boy," Mr. Caw was saying. "I didn't mean to get him into any trouble or make him feel bad. If we were younger, we'd take him, be foster parents, you know, but we're getting too old for that. I tried to give him some advice a couple of times, but I think it all turned out to be wrong. I'm afraid I made it worse for him, not better. He doesn't want to just come and visit at our house, he wants to find somebody who loves him enough to give him a real home."

"I know." Miss Susan's voice was soft. "I'm not supposed to have favorites among the children, but Eddie's mine, and it's not just because he's been here the longest. He's really a very dear little boy."

Mr. Caw sighed. "Well, I thought I'd ought to tell you. That I realized after I got him over to my place that he was hoping we'd keep him, you know. He's hurt and disappointed. And now I understand you're planning to leave, and he's very fond of you. He's pretty upset, I'm afraid."

"Yes. Most of the children who come here are upset, of course, because they've lost the people closest to them, or been abandoned by them. Eddie's lost twice already; first his mother deserted him, and then his grandmother died. And today his best friend here went away, and I think the Castles will be keeping Jonas. They don't have him, officially, as a foster child, but Mr. Castle thought they'd make an application. Which leaves Eddie very much alone."

They went inside, then, and Eddie couldn't hear them any more. He didn't want to listen, anyway. Nothing they were saying made him feel any better. What good was it that they all liked him if nobody *wanted* him?

Well, if he couldn't go in the front door, maybe he'd try a window. He retraced his steps and looked around for something to climb on to reach the dining room windows. All he had to do was remove a screen, and he could get in that way.

He found a stepladder Mr. Linders had forgotten to put away when he'd washed the windows and climbed to the top of it and unfastened the screen. As he crawled forward through the window, the ladder rocked backward and fell onto the grass, out of reach.

If he wanted to get out this way, he'd have to jump to the ground. With his luck, he'd probably break his leg and have a cast on that as well as on his arm, he thought. Eddie crept through the swinging door into the kitchen.

He didn't often get a chance to visit it when it was empty. Sometimes, on Sunday, Cook fixed lunch in advance and left it in the big refrigerators. Mrs. Mundy would put it out when it was time. Otherwise, Mrs. Mundy would sit in the living room with her feet up and read or watch television, or talk on the phone to her daughter. It had struck Eddie as peculiar when he learned that Mrs. Mundy had a daughter. She didn't seem like anybody's mother.

Today the kitchen was silent except for the hum of the refrigerators. He peeked into the first one and saw the sandwiches, already made up and wrapped in plastic. There were bowls of red Jell-O and individual dishes of carrot-raisin salad. Hmm, Eddie thought. Carrot-raisin was his favorite. Maybe he'd wait until at least after lunch to run away.

In fact, he decided, it would probably take a while to collect enough food to live on until he found a place to live. He decided there wasn't much in the refrigerator that he could use; it wouldn't keep long enough. Except for cheese, maybe. He cut a generous chunk off the large block of cheese and wrapped it in foil from the box in a drawer.

In the pantry he selected a box of crackers and a package of oatmeal cookies and two cans of tuna fish. That meant he had to have a can opener, too, so he got one and put it in his pocket. What else, Eddie wondered? And where was he going to hide everything until he was ready to leave?

It had better be outside the house, he reasoned. That would make it easier to get at when the time came. He twisted the button that unlocked the back door, made sure that no one could see him, and began to carry his loot outside to put it under the porch, where he usually kept a book or some other small treasure.

He couldn't carry much at a time with one arm in a cast, so he had to make a number of trips. When he'd finished, he was pleased at how much he'd gathered. There were canned peaches and apricots and apple juice and more cartons of cookies. There was also a yellow plastic bucket of peanut butter, and he'd remembered to bring a knife to spread it.

The more he looked at it, however, the more unlikely it seemed that he could carry it all very far. Especially with only one good arm.

Still, it made him feel better to know he had supplies if he needed them.

Miss Susan and Mr. Caw were gone when he finally walked out through the front door. Well, he might as well get used to that. Pretty soon there wouldn't be anyone left that he cared about at all.

Over the next few days Eddie kept trying to think of where to go when he ran away. Since he wasn't quite ready yet, he played with the other boys in the cardboard and scrap-lumber fort. At first Arnie said he couldn't play because he hadn't helped to build it, but Barry said that didn't matter. The others agreed, so Eddie became first one of the Indians who attacked the fort, then one of the soldiers fighting inside.

The next day they learned that Lonnie was going into a foster home where there were already two other children, one a boy his own age.

Lonnie was excited and happy, and Eddie tried to be happy for him, too.

Dick's and Cheryl's aunt was coming from California to get them, so they packed their things and got ready for an airplane ride. Neither of them had ever been in an airplane, and they were so excited they couldn't think about anything else.

Even Arnie had been told that he'd be going home in another week. His parents were out of the hospital and there was a nurse coming to stay with them for a while. Eddie felt strange when Arnie said, "Hey, I think I'm going to miss you guys."

Several times Miss Susan tried to talk to Eddie, but he always made some excuse and got away. He didn't want to hear what she had to say. If she wanted to marry some old fiancé and go away forever, she could go ahead and do it. He didn't want her to tell him any more about it.

He'd always liked Jenny, but now all she could talk about was the upcoming wedding. Jenny was going to wear a blue dress and carry flowers, and Eddie didn't see how she could talk about just *that* for hours.

Miss Susan's replacement was a Mrs. Paulson, who worked with Miss Susan every day in the office, learning what she would have to do. Though she wasn't as pretty as Miss Susan, she seemed nice enough, to everybody but Eddie. Even though she spoke to him kindly and smiled, he knew he'd never like her as much as he liked Miss Susan.

"Eddie, you *are* going to be ring bearer for us, aren't you?" Miss Susan asked when she was finally able to corner him for a minute.

He scowled. "Not if I have to wear short pants like those sissy ring bearers in the movies."

"No, of course not. You can wear the clothes you wear to Sunday School. Eddie, I'd like to talk with you, privately. Could you come into my office now, while Mrs. Paulson is out to lunch?"

"I don't have time to talk now," Eddie said rudely, and walked away before she could stop him.

He'd made up his mind, now, for sure. He'd stay for the wedding, and then he would take what he could carry of the supplies from under the back porch, and he'd start walking. Somewhere out there in the wide world must be those people Miss Susan had said would want him, someday. All he had to do was find them.

Dick and Cheryl came to tell him goodbye. "We can't take everything on the plane, Aunt Laura says, so I'm leaving my wagon here," Dick said. "I guess I'm getting too big to pull a wagon, anyway. So you can have it, Eddie, unless you want to give it to one of the little kids."

Eddie felt a stirring of excitement. A wagon would carry a lot more than he could carry in one good arm and his sling. "Thanks," Eddie told him.

He had to tear off a few more strips of the lattice boards under the porch to make room for it, but he managed to get the wagon under there and loaded it up. The food supply didn't look as large once it was in the wagon, so Eddie added more things to it. More crackers, and just before he left he'd get a loaf of bread, maybe. He got a blanket and a pillow, too, from the upstairs hall closet, which he put over the top of everything else.

He was ready. If it made him sort of scared to think about actually starting down the road, why, he told himself that he'd get over it once he saw that nothing bad happened to him. At least he *hoped* nothing bad would happen.

The week of the wedding, two new boys came. Their names were Frank and Donald, and their hair was almost white. Towheads, Mrs. Mundy called them. Frank had the bed next to Eddie, where Jonas had slept, and he kept asking Eddie questions. Eddie knew the answers, so he didn't mind answering. It kept his mind off other things. But finally the day of the wedding came.

Everybody got dressed up. Mrs. Mundy had a new dress, and so did Cook, and Miss Susan was going to wear a long white dress with lace on it.

"She looks so beautiful!" Jenny breathed, clasping her hands at her chest. "And she wants to talk to you, Eddie. She said to please send you up to Mrs. Mundy's room, where she's getting ready."

"I don't want to talk to her," Eddie said. "It's bad enough I have to carry a stupid little pillow with a ring on it."

Instead of going to Miss Susan, he crept around the corner of the house and checked on his supplies. The wagon was loaded, including the loaf of bread, which he had added that morning.

When they were all busy after the ceremony, eating cake and drinking lemonade and champagne, he would slip away. Probably nobody would even notice he was gone for a long time, and he'd be miles away.

He got his hands dirty, crawling under the porch to look, so he'd have to go inside again to wash them. The scowl was getting so deep on Eddie's face that it felt permanent.

There were people all over the place, in summery dresses and shirts. Many of them he didn't know, friends of Miss Susan's who didn't live or work at the home. Nobody paid any attention to him as he raced up the stairs and into the bathroom. There was dirt on his cast, too, so he thought he'd better do something to clean it off or it would look terrible when he carried the blue satin pillow with the ring on it.

Unfortunately, the dirt didn't come off the cast, it simply smeared. It looked worse now than it had to begin with. Eddie stared at it in dismay. He'd disgrace Miss Susan, and himself, if he joined the wedding party looking so grubby.

What, then?

Eddie remembered the big white shoes that Mrs. Mundy usually wore. Except for the time the jelly had squirted all over them, they had always been very white. She must polish them to keep them that way, he decided.

He crossed from the boys bathroom to the one Mrs. Mundy had all to herself and began to look through the cabinet under the sink. Ah, there it was! White shoe polish!

It was awkward, peeling off his sling and putting on the polish with the little brush, and it covered up most of the autographs. Eddie painted around the blue letters printed by Mr. Caw and decided the rest of it looked fine. The only trouble was that he'd used all the shoe polish. Mrs. Mundy would wonder where it went, and he didn't have any money to buy her another bottle.

Well, he wouldn't be around when she discovered it was gone. Eddie started to open the door and then heard the voices outside in the hallway and in the adjoining bedroom.

"Please, Patrick, see if you can find him! I have to talk to Eddie before this goes any further," Miss Susan said, and she sounded very worried. "He promised me he'd carry the ring, and I haven't been able to speak to him since. He's avoiding me, and now that Arnie's discovered a wagon and groceries and blankets hidden under the porch—they have to be Eddie's. I know he's planning to take them and run away!"

Eddie didn't recognize the deep male voice that answered. "Listen, I know the groom isn't supposed to see the bride before the ceremony, but if this kid is in trouble, maybe we'd better forget that particular tradition and get working on this together. Talking to each other through a door isn't going to work if we really have to make a search."

"I'm not going to get married until we've found Eddie and talked to him," Miss Susan said. "I'll wait here, Patrick, and please hurry. It's almost time to go downstairs."

It made Eddie feel strange, so strange that he forgot he was holding the shoe polish bottle. All of a sudden it slid right out of his fingers and smashed on the edge of the sink.

He had thought it was empty, but there was enough polish left so that it splattered over his shoes and the tile floor, and he looked down at it in despair. What was the matter with him, that he was always breaking or spilling something?

The two doors came open at the same time, the one into Mrs. Mundy's bedroom and the one from the hallway. Miss Susan, looking so beautiful she was like an angel, stood in one doorway, and her fiancé stood in the other one.

"Eddie! Where have you been? What are you doing in here?" Miss Susan demanded.

The fiancé named Patrick spoke in the deep voice of a big man. "Looks to me he's cleaned up his cast with shoe polish, right, Eddie?"

When Eddie looked up, he was astonished. Patrick had red hair, almost the same color as Eddie's, and lots of freckles. He didn't look ugly, though; he was wearing a dark suit and was quite handsome.

"It slipped," Eddie said. "And broke."

"Never mind. We'll clean it up later," Miss Susan decided. "Tell them we'll be right there, Patrick. I need just a minute to talk to Eddie."

Patrick grinned. "OK. See you downstairs." And then, to Eddie's amazement, he winked.

"He's the one you're going to marry?" Eddie asked.

"Yes, he's Patrick. Eddie, come in here for a minute and listen to me. Please."

She took his good hand and led him out of the bathroom; they both sat down on the edge of Mrs. Mundy's bed. "I've been trying and trying to talk to you, Eddie, and you wouldn't let me. It's important."

Eddie stiffened his back, braced for whatever the bad news was going to be, wondering how much of a fuss Mrs. Mundy would make over the broken bottle and all that glass scattered over her bathroom.

"Never mind that," Miss Susan said. She was still holding onto his hand, and she bent toward him, her face serious. "Eddie, you know you've been my favorite of all the children here, in the four years I've worked at Riverside Children's Home. I cared a lot for you, but I didn't realize how much until I knew I was going to go away and I wouldn't be seeing you again. Patrick and I have talked about having a family of our own, but I didn't know how he'd react to having a ready-made family, so I couldn't speak to you until I'd had a chance to discuss it with Patrick. Eddie, I told him all about you—"

Eddie stared at her, unable to keep the anger and hurt from his face. "You, too," he said. "Just like Mr. Caw. Everybody has to tell everybody about me."

When he tried to pull his hand away, she wouldn't let him. "Wait, Eddie, let me finish. I told Patrick, and he says you're just the way he was when he was nine years old. He thinks it would be wonderful to have a foster-son. Do you understand? We want you to go with us, when we move away to a new home."

For a minute Eddie didn't believe it. Go to live with Miss Susan and her new husband? To stay?

He couldn't think of anything to say. Miss Susan laughed and hugged him. "I mean it, Eddie. We want you to be our son. Will you?"

His voice sounded very gruff. "I guess so," he said.

Miss Susan sprang to her feet. "Come on, now, here's the pillow, and here's the box with the ring, and it's time for us to go."

Eddie moved as if he were in a dream. He carried the silly little blue satin pillow with the ring on it, and he listened to the minister say the words that made Miss Susan and Patrick man and wife. And when Patrick's eye caught Eddie's, Patrick grinned again.

After the ceremony was over, everybody

laughed and talked and ate cake. It wasn't chocolate, but it was pretty good, anyway, Eddie thought. His piece had three roses and a leaf on it.

There was a long table piled high with presents, wrapped in pretty paper with elegant bows and ribbons. And then Eddie turned when he heard a familiar bark.

The Caws were coming toward him through the crowd, and in front of them raced F.G.P. with a white satin bow tied to his collar. The dog leaped joyfully at Eddie, almost knocking him down.

"Well," Mr. Caw said, "I understand you took my advice, boy, and it worked."

He was smiling, and so was Mrs. Caw. "What advice was that?" Mrs. Caw wanted to know.

"I told him to decide who was the most important person to please and make her like him. Looks like that's what he's done."

Miss Susan looked up, laughing, from the table where she and Patrick were unwrapping toasters and towels and china plates and saucers. "I've loved Eddie for a long time. It wasn't until Mr. Caw talked to me that I realized how

much. I'm very happy that Patrick agrees with me."

The bridegroom looked at F.G.P., who was licking Eddie's face as the boy crouched at the dog's level. "Does that ribbon on the dog mean what I think it does?"

"Seemed like a good present," Mr. Caw said cheerfully, "for a couple starting off married life with a nine-year-old boy. What do you think?"

For a moment Miss Susan had a funny look on her face, and then she began to laugh. "He's a lovely wedding present," she agreed. "Only would it be too much to ask that you keep him and Eddie until we get back from our honeymoon?"

"Two weeks?" Mrs. Caw asked, and Eddie looked anxiously up at her. Her blue eyes twinkled. "I think I'm young enough to hold up with a boy and a dog for that long. Particularly since we're going to take our vacation at the lake for the rest of this month."

Eddie's good arm tightened around F.G.P. until the dog yelped. Eddie looked at Mr. Caw and saw the painter's wink, and he spoke in a low voice that the others didn't hear.

"Maybe," Eddie said, "he really is a fairy godpuppy, after all. Do you think so?"

"I wouldn't be surprised," Mr. Caw said. "I wouldn't be surprised at all."

F.G.P. barked and wagged his tail. Eddie thought it was a pretty good wedding except for when he'd had to carry the ring on the little pillow, and he hoped they wouldn't waste too much time on the honeymoon. The sooner *that* was over, the sooner he'd have his family.

And until then, he thought happily, he'd have F.G.P.

He wondered what else a fairy godpuppy could be expected to do for him.